13

THE ACTION

Peter Tonkin

This title world edition published in Great Britain 1996 by
SEVERN HOUSE PUBLISHERS LTD of
9–15 High Street, Sutton, Surrey SM1 1DF.
First published in the USA 1996 by
SEVERN HOUSE PUBLISHERS INC of
595 Madison Avenue, New York, NY 10022.

British Library Cataloguing in Publication Data
Tonkin, Peter, 1950–
    The action
    1. English Fiction – 20th century
    I. Title
    823.9'14 [F]

    ISBN 0-7278-4983-2

Typeset by Hewer Text Composition Services, Edinburgh.
Printed and bound in Great Britain by
Hartnolls Ltd, Bodmin, Cornwall.

Contents

Part One

Prologue

Chapter One

Washington

Washington D.C., November 1997

"So," said the Secretary of State, "what we have at the beginning of this action is a sunken ship suddenly surrounded by the four largest Intelligence Services in the world, and you don't know why." The Secretary leaned belligerently across the open folder of case notes on his desk. A trick of the light threw light over the lenses of his glasses so that his eyes were invisible to the man seated opposite him. This man, Abe Parmilee, folded his hands in his lap and leaned back into the spindly chair until it creaked. Parmilee was a huge man, and he gave the impression of being a slow thinker. He was not. He paused carefully before answering the Secretary's challenge. When he spoke, it was with a soft Mid-West accent which seemed to come from his boots. "No, Mr Secretary," he said. "That's not quite the way I see it." He paused again. There was absolute silence in the big, bookfilled room. Outside it was pouring and blowing half a gale, but here the wind and rain made no impression. They were in the basement of the White House, in the Secretary of State's private office, near the tiny press room, where Harry Truman's swimming-pool used to be. "It seems to me," continued Parmilee after a moment, "that this is all tied up with the earlier intelligence action in Singapore and Hong Kong."

The Secretary nodded once, light glinting on the pale waves of his perfect hair. "The attempted defection of the man Feng," he said.

"Yes, sir, that is correct." Parmilee spoke slowly and quietly, his voice like the rumble of a distant earthquake. Every now and then his huge square hands, their backs spotted with orange freckles and forested with what looked like copper fuse-wire, would take flight as he spoke.

The Secretary sat, enthralled, as the tale of violence, confusion and international deviousness began to unfold. And as he listened, his own mind whirled along with Parmilee's, filling in blanks, strengthening speculation, building up something that he needed very badly. Very badly indeed.

A few weeks earlier, the Secertary had gone to China. His visit was designed to smooth the way for the President's visit before Christmas. The Secretary of State, a man of some standing in the diplomatic world, a bargainer on the international circuit second to none, a hard man and a rough rider, had been given a chilly reception by the Chinese. This reception had extended into an icy stay, with everything, it seemed, carefully designed to border on the insulting. The Secretary, unprepared, had been at first surprised and then enraged. Ultimately, however, he had come away concerned. Whereas on the surface the desire for detente with the United States seemed to be real enough, the National Peoples' Conference in January had thrown a lot of hard liners into the forefront of Chinese politics. And the Chairman, growing very old now, seemed to be relaxing his grip a little. The result had been humiliating for the Secretary and embarrassing for his country. This was not his main concern, however.

4

He was worried about the future, about December, and the President's visit.

The Secretary had come away from Beijing with the definite impression that what had happened to him was going to happen to the President also. And that, of course, would not be merely embarrassing: it would be a disaster. And yet the President had set his mind on going. It would be a diplomatic coup of some weight, and the President deemed it necessary to his political strength at home that he be given the chance to sparkle abroad. There had been more budget clashes with the Senate. Government offices had been closed again. The President needed to sparkle.

"You'll think of something," he had said to the Secretary the evening before in the Oval office. "I know you well enough, Mr Secretary, to be sure that you will come up with something." And he smiled cheerfully as he walked out of the door with his aides. As soon as the door had closed and the footsteps began to move away down the marble hall, the Secretary of State sat at the President's desk, leaning back against the leather of the big chair, still warm from the President's back. He had looked across the littered desktop at the Director of Central Intelligence. "It's not going to be easy."

The Director rose and stretched until his joints creaked. "They gave me a very rough ride over there," continued the Secretary grimly, tapping the point home on every syllable with a perfectly manicured fingernail against the leather desktop. "Since the National People's Conference in January, and with the Chairman getting old, they're all trying to prove what great hard-liners they are." The Director sat down again and studied his mud-marked black shoes. Rain had rattled against glass; dead leaves had wheeled through the bright beams outside the Oval office windows. According to the makeshift weather forecast, it would improve – therefore everyone was certain it would actually be worse tomorrow. The weather bureau had been hit with the rest of the Government offices.

"They gave me the roughest ride I've ever had, bar none," the Secretary repeated, looking at the closed door as if the President still lingered there. "They're setting themselves up to take him to pieces," he persisted, "politically as well as economically. Now they have Hong Kong . . ."

The Director of Central Intelligence had spoken at last: "We can't allow that," he said.

"Right! Correct! Russia is just in the right mood to make some good sound political capital out of any egg he gets on his face. They have so many problems at home, they're in the same boat as us. And this administration can't take a lot. Certainly it can't take a hatchet job done publicly on the President as soon as he sets foot in Beijing."

The Director of Central Intelligence had stirred, removing his glasses to massage his eyes under frowning, worried brows. "The Company's credit isn't that good at the moment either here or abroad. You know that."

"I don't want credit. I don't want diplomatic weight. I don't want anything anyone has ever heard about." The Secretary's hand had struck down like a snake behind a pile of books and had come up with the National Intelligence Daily. "I don't want anything that's been in here," he said, crushing it as though it were *Pravda* or *Isvestia* instead of the daily update on important events within the CIA circulated only to the 50 men with absolute security clearance, who needed to know everything.

"Tall order," the DCI had observed, carefully.

"Too tall?"

"No, I don't think so. I'll have a word with my National

6

Intelligence Officer for China, but there were some things going on over the summer. I think the man you want to see is Parmilee from Plans. Far East Division."

The Secretary of State's eyes had narrowed. "If there was an intelligence action in the Far East over the summer, I should have heard about it," he pointed out.

"There hasn't been a full report yet," the DCI had said, shifting position carefully in the chair. "We're still trying to work out precisely what happened." There had been a little silence, and then he had continued, "It looks a bit like two covert actions, but it might have been only one. Really, we don't know anything about what was going on. It looked like a defection to begin with, but then it all went haywire. After that it was just one long shambles rounded out with an earthquake."

"An earthquake?" the Secretary had asked carefully, in case this was another piece of the never-ending jargon which litters the vocabulary of intelligence men.

"Yes," the Director had said. "An earthquake." He had moved his hands to signify the quaking of the earth.

The Secretary of State had shrugged, leaned back in the chair behind the President's desk, made a steeple of his hands and said, "You think there's something in all this we can use against the Chinese if the going gets really rough in Beijing?"

"I really couldn't say what is in there and what is not. Talk to the case officer. Talk to Parmilee." A lull in the conversation had been filled by the rattling of the windows. "It depends what you want," the DCI had said.

"I want an edge," the Secretary of State had answered decidedly. "I want an ace in the hole. What was it Teddy Roosevelt said? 'Speak softly and carry a bit of stick.' Well that's what I want. I want the biggest god-damned stick I can lay my hands on."

*   *   *

7

Thus it was that Abe Parmilee, a senior man in the Far East Section of the Plans Division, found himself in the Secretary's office in the basement of the White House late the next evening, trying to tie it all together – the defection of Feng, the disappearance of the ship *Wanderer*, the carnage, the earthquake, the confusion. Both men, having talked it through twice, admitted to a gut feeling that there was something important there. Neither man could put his finger on it. After Parmilee finished speaking there was a silence, then they began to skirt around it once again. The Secretary opened a red file of white flimsies which were the field reports on the first action. Or the *first* part of *the* action – if Parmilee was right and it all held together.

"You thought this man Feng was the genuine article?" he asked. "I thought defections went out with flares and the Osmonds."

Parmilee leaned forward again, spade palms on tree-trunk thighs. "We weren't sure. We got the news through Hong Kong Local Station, if you could call the tiny office the Brits used to allow us out there a Station. That's all. The National Intelligence Officer with responsibility for China had heard of him, though no one at Plans had. We just got the message that he was coming out and it was too good to miss. Those were the last days before it all went back to China, remember, so we acted fast. One of our ships, the *Lincoln*, was in the China Sea. We sent it to Hong Kong immediately and I briefed Ed Lydecker, from the Operations section of the Office of Current Intelligence, and sent him out to the ship with orders to debrief Feng on board and bring him back."

"You didn't want Hong Kong Local Station to do it?"

"No. They were just a couple of guys in loud suits anyway.

We'd been pulling out as fast as the banks and the triads. They were to bring him through the city and put him on the *Lincoln*. I didn't want them to debrief him."

The evening dragged on. Coffee was brought every hour or so and they drank most of it. Outside, the gale howled in spite of the weather forecast. Once in a while, Parmilee found his mind wandering to thoughts of his tiny Chinese wife alone in their house in Georgetown.

At last the Secretary sat back and closed both the folders. "So," he said, "what we have is a pair of intelligence actions. First action: a defection from China into Hong Kong. It goes wrong. The subject, Feng, disappears. He reappears a few hours later in Singapore. He disappears again. Action terminated. Several dead. Probable authors of deaths two Chinese agents code-named Hummingbird and Bee. Hong Kong, Singapore, then nothing. How did you read it again?"

"It seemed to be either a strike at Hong Kong Local Station, complete with trick defection to bring them out into the open. Or it was a genuine defection and we lost him. Either would make sense and it was all falling apart out there, remember."

"Yes," said the Secretary. "I think it was genuine though. I think these people, the Hummingbird and the Bee, took him back from Singapore. But if this is so, then what is going on six weeks later with the British ship, the *Wanderer*, sinking in the middle of the Indian Ocean?"

"That was the only place Feng went in Singapore. To that ship, the *Wanderer*," said Parmilee, his great, square red-freckled hand sweeping back through his thin, wiry red hair. "That's why I set the *Lincoln* to shadowing her. It was all I had left. A hunch . . ."

"OK. We have this British ship, which had been visited in Singapore by a defecting Chinese government official, sinking with almost all hands in the middle of the Indian Ocean, and all hell breaks loose. I know why we were involved: we were shadowing it. But the Chinese?"

"They were shadowing too."

Because maybe friend Feng put something on the *Wanderer* while he was on board," mused the Secretary. "His bargaining counter. They usually bring a bargaining counter, don't they – information, something like that?"

"Yes," said Parmilee. "And when he knew Hummingbird and Bee were onto him, he stashed it, whatever it was, in case they caught him."

"But why a *British* ship?" asked the Secretary.

"Chance?" said Parmilee, his bright Irish-blue eyes flicking restlessly round the room, not believing the word.

"OK. Leave that for a moment," said the Secretary. "What about the KGB? Why did they get mixed up in it?"

Parmilee shrugged. "They're not the KGB any more. They have been the Federal Security Service for a couple of years now. But you're right, they must have been well motivated," he said. "They've been keeping their heads down since Chechnya. And it was Andropov himself."

"The British?"

Parmilee shook his head. "It was a British ship," he said. "Someone pulled a string on the Old Boy network. You know how the Brits are."

"So. We're back to the beginning", the Secretary persisted. "What we have is a sunken ship, suddenly surrounded by the four largest intelligence services in the world. It's the Cold War in the Indian Ocean for Christ's sake. And you don't know why."

"I don't think anyone knew precisely why," said Parmilee

reasonably, not for the first time, frowning at the use of that old-fashioned phrase "Cold War".

"I see. So what were you all going to do – you, the British, the Russian and the Chinese? I mean once the survivors from the ship had found the island, and *you* had found the island and everyone was sitting there in the middle of the Indian Ocean armed to the teeth and staring at each other. What were you actually going to do?"

"Find out what it was all about," explained Parmilee. He moved his huge frame to a position of relative comfort on the small hard chair, looking at the Secretary's pensive profile. "Our field agent, Lydecker. He's a good man. He would have sorted it out in no time, flat."

"The only person who seems to have had any idea what was going on was that big Englishman, Stone . . . I wish he'd been with us instead of . . ." he drifted into silence, then he roused himself. "Still. There's no blame to be attached when it falls to pieces like this one did."

Parmilee agreed.

"I wouldn't have liked to have been on that island," said the Secretary.

"Me neither," said Parmilee.

The Secretary of State made a steeple out of his forearms and hands, resting his elbows on the arms of his chair, rocking his face forward until his thumbnails were on his teeth and his index fingers against his glasses at the bridge of his nose. He thought for a while. Eventually he looked up. "You haven't got case names for these actions," he said.

"No, sir. We don't."

"Siva and Kali," said the Secretary. "Indian gods of death, rebirth, death and destruction."

"Very apt," said Parmilee. "There was enough death and destruction. And a hell of a lot of thugs, too, at one time or another. And India, of course."

11

Silence returned. Then the Secretary of State said, "It's in there somewhere. Somewhere between the defection and the earthquake, between Siva and Kali. I feel it. It is *in* there!"

"What is?" asked Parmilee.

"The diplomatic stick with which I am going to guard the President's back next month in Beijing."

Silence returned. Parmilee's thoughts wandered towards Wei-Wei his wife alone in their huge bed. The Secretary thought of less alluring Orientals. Coffee came and he said, "Right. Let's take it from the top again."

Chapter Two

Prelude: Siva

Hong Kong, Far East, June 1997

To the north of Hong Kong between Kowloon and China there lies a bustling, mountainous district leased from the Chinese for 99 years in 1898. Only the British would still be calling this the New Territories in the year it was to be returned to China.

Feng came out through the New Territories on the night of 25 June. How he managed to cross the border and avoid the Ghurka patrols which range the hills in the dark, nobody knew. He was picked up, as agreed, on the outskirts of Kowloon just after dawn on the 26th by four men from the depleted CIA Local Station. Feng was a tall man, unusually tall for a Chinese, and he towered head and shoulders above the crowd bustling off to work. He was nervous. Every movement betrayed the tension in his long, lean body. Fenderman, the senior field operative, CIA Local Station, shrugged himself off the wall and plunged into the colourful crowd as soon as the tall defector caught his eye. A few yards back down the road, he knew, Albertson and Burke would have swung invisibly into the tail position. Ahead, Mathews should be ready to join the parade. They were more or less all of the station men left now. And they would be gone in a week.

Fenderman was short. His skin was sallow. His hair was black and oiled back flat on his skull. Thick pebble glasses magnified narrow brown eyes. He had been on various Far East stations since he first joined the Company. He was dressed in a suit almost cut to a Western style in a shiny sky blue, white pinstripe material. The pinstripes went from side to side instead of up and down. He was clutching in his plump right hand a bright bag bearing the legend of a big store on the Wanchai end of Queen's Road. He did not stand out in the crowd.

His shoulder brushed Feng's upper arm. No words were exchanged. Feng took the bag. Inside it were a change of clothes, a wallet with identity papers, some money and a Gold AmEx credit card: a simple survival kit – as agreed.

Keeping Feng's head in view, Fenderman began to fall back as soon as he had relinquished the bag. His eyes darted among the faces of the crown around him, looking for Albertson and Burke. They were new men, sent out to Hong Kong Station a few weeks before only to get a bit of experience while there was still time. This was their first big job. Fenderman wanted to make sure they did not mess it up – especially with the big man from Langley, Virginia, sitting on board the *Lincoln* in the harbour waiting for them. And the end of a posting was like the end of a movie, the bit that everyone remembered.

Lydecker had been unhappy, but his orders from Parmilee had been specific: Local Station would bring Feng in. After all, the guys were there to learn some bush-craft. Lydecker would get him as soon as he set foot on the *Lincoln* and not before. The tall, rangy operative had made it quite clear to Fenderman's boss, the Chief of Station, that if anything went wrong there would be severe reprisals: no cushy postings, no extended leave when the Station closed next week. The Chief of Station had passed the buck down to Fenderman as smartly as he could. Feng was important, the Chief had said, a gift from God and probably the best they were going to get. There were to be no mistakes.

Fenderman's eyes stared over the oriental countenances all around. Millions and millions of people lived in the city – most of them seemed to be here, now. With a growing feeling of rage he began to realize that Albertson and Burke were not among them. It never once occurred to him that anything was wrong. He just thought a couple of green kids had messed it up. He actually thought to himself, "I will have their guts . . ." when the screaming started behind him.

Fenderman saw Feng hesitate and swing round to look back. He realized that he himself was the only person in the crowd who was not looking back. He was in the act of turning when Burke's hand fell on his arm. "Burke!" he said, "where in Hell . . ." Burke's eyes and mouth were wide. His callow face was utterly white. With enormous effort he said, "Head . . ." His knees gave, and suddenly he was clutching Fenderman's thigh. "Head *ache*," he said to the sky-blue white-lined trousers, and then he fell forward. From under his short intensely black hair something protruded. Something shiny. Fenderman, sickened, knew what it was. It was the end of a bicycle spoke. Someone had placed a sharpened bicycle spoke at the point where the neck joins the skull, just above the 'atlas', or first cervical vertebra, and then driven it up into Burke's brain.

"Oh, my God!" said Fenderman. He looked up. There was screaming, still, from a little farther down the road. Fenderman yelled in elegant Cantonese, "I'm a doctor!" Then he said it again in heavily accented English, and shouldered forward. But of course Albertson, like Burke, needed a mortician, not a GP On his knees beside the young man's corpse, Fenderman thought, "I hope Mathews has his eye on Feng." Then he stood up. "There is nothing I can do

15

here," he said. "This man is dead." The crowd involuntarily surged backwards, as he knew it would, and he used the motion to cover his escape before the khaki-clad Crown Colony Police could arrive on the scene.

He went down the road as fast as he could, calling "Police! Police!" to cover the fact that he was moving against the stream. Beyond the edge of the crowd, the road was suddenly empty except for a beggar asleep against a wall. Fenderman stopped, mopped his face which was suddenly covered with sweat in the warm, dazzling morning, cleaned his pebble glasses and looked around. There was no sign of Feng. "Mathews," he muttered to himself, "you had better have him in your sights!" He walked swiftly down the road, his mind full of what Lydecker was going to say even if Mathews was still with Feng, which looked less and less likely now. Visions of the tall agent's lean face dark with righteous rage rose unbidden to Fenderman's brain and blocked out his sight until he was at least 15 yards past the sleeping beggar, and then some trick of visual memory made him realize that the beggar's feet protruding from beneath a ragged blanket were pale and uncalloused. "Oh *no!*" he whispered, turning back. Closer investigation showed the ragged blanket to be covering a good suit. This was no sleeping beggar. This was Mathews and he was never going to wake up.

Oddly enough, to Fenderman's way of thinking, Lydecker reacted more with sorrow than with anger. He sat the shaken little man down in his stateroom on the *Lincoln* with a lot of sympathy and bourbon. The Chief came in, white with shock, his face reminding Fenderman of Burke with the bicycle spoke in his head. There was nothing they could do, so they sat around and stared at each other while the Crown Colony Police started their investigation. A rumpled, square man called Hannegan, pilot of the Bell helicopter lashed to the landing-pad on the *Lincoln's* broad bow, joined them silently with more bourbon.

"The British aren't going to like this," mourned the Chief. "A final blot on the copybook. They only let us run it as a final favour."

"The British!" exploded Fenderman. "Hell! *I* don't like it!"

Water lapped the sheer metal side. A circle of light from a porthole moved infinitesimally as the *Lincoln* rocked and the sun climbed.

"Bicycle spokes," said Lydecker. "I've come across those before." All their eyes turned towards his lanky figure sprawled uneasily in a comfortable chair. His black hair was tousled. His shirt was open at the neck, revealing a virile mat of curls. His sharp amber eyes lost focus and drifted down until he was studying his gleaming black Oxfords as he thought. He had the practised field agent's ability to extract important points, like splinters of shattered bone, from the mess of mayhem.

It had all been included in the emergency interim report sent in code to Parmilee, case officer, in CIA headquarters, Langley. There was nothing more they could do. "Shouldn't we be on the street, *looking*?" said the Chief. Lydecker's amber eyes rested on him for a second, then went to Hannegan and Fenderman. Nobody answered. The dead-end office in Boise, Idaho, rose in the Chief of Station's mind. He fell silent. Half an hour later, just as midday was threatening, a message came back from Parmilee. Feng had used his Gold AmEx card. As soon as it was presented, its number was fed into the credit company's computer together with the cost of the transaction, its full details and its location. The number on Feng's card triggered an alert. A message was automatically sent to another

17

computer. Suddenly a printout in the CIA headquarters in Langley, Virginia, began to reveal facts about financial matters being transacted half a world away.

The credit card had been presented at 08.25 local time at the booking counter at Kai Tak airport. With it, Feng had bought a ticket on a flight to Singapore.

Singapore

Feng caught the Jumbo out of Kai Tak at 0900 in the morning, local time. It stopped over in Bangkok and landed in Singapore at 1405 that afternoon. Without luggage, and with an excellently forged passport which proclaimed him to be the owner of a chain of exclusive Chinese restaurants in San Francisco, and an American citizen, Feng came out of Changi airport at 1420, while most of the other passengers from his flight were still caught up at the barriers inevitable in any international entrepôt. It was an overcast, humid afternoon in Singapore. Everyone was moving as slowly as possible: he stood out from the crowd, not only because of his height, but because of the urgency of his movements. Fenderman had given him white trainers, blue jeans, a white shirt and a lightweight denim jacket, all of which he was wearing. The jacket had huge dark stains at the armpits. He was still clutching the bag from the store in the Wanchai district of Hong Kong.

The men from the CIA's little Singapore Station had no difficulty in locating him. They followed his bright taxi in their black Mercedes Benz. None of them left the car or ventured on foot alone onto the busy streets after they had followed him out from Changi's Arrivals Hall. As well as the flight number, and a description of the man they were to meet, the messages from Agent Lydecker in Hong Kong and

18

Case Officer Parmilee in Langley had warned of the possible presence of two Chinese agents, code-named Hummingbird and Bee, who were almost certainly responsible for three deaths on Hong Kong station. These agents, known only by their modus operandi – sharpenened bicycle spokes – were deadly and no risks should be taken as there was a strong possibility that they were still on Feng's heels. Lydecker himself would arrive on the 1615 flight out of Kai Tak.

This flight was the direct 747, and it landed at Changi Airport at 1830. By then Feng had disappeared again.

At 1421 on 26 June, therefore, the tall Chinese in the bright blue, easily-visible clothes, raised his right arm, flapping the Wanchai bag like a red flag, to summon the yellow taxi. As he did so, the two rear doors of the black Mercedes opened together, and the two agents who had followed him across the Arrivals Hall, dumped themselves silently on the soft bench seat. The car grumbled into motion as the taxi performed a dangerous U-turn and sped away down towards the city. Following the colourful taxi was easy. The three silent agents all watched it together, their Chief of Station having put it to them very plainly that he did not wish to end up in the same position as his idiot counterpart in Hong Kong. The driver employed no tricks or devices beloved of theoreticians in the art of shadowing. He kept the front bumper of the black Mercedes close to the rear bumper of the yellow taxi at all times, and hang the consequences.

They went through the perfectly clipped public gardens over the bridge spanning the Rochore River and into the bright, busy thoroughfare of Victoria Street. The first time the taxi stopped, with the Mercedes close behind, both black back doors were half open – in spite of orders – before it became obvious that the cab was waiting, and Feng had just popped into a Bank to change some of Fenderman's money. After that the taxi stopped every 20 minutes or so, and Feng would vanish into a shop. He never seemed to buy much. There were hardly ever any large packages, although the Wanchai bag stopped flapping emptily.

The afternoon wore on. Everyone in the black Mercedes got very bored. The only thing they could be certain that Feng had bought was a copy of the *Straits Times*. Everything else was either wrapped or put straight into the bag. It grew hotter and hotter. The back of Feng's jacket, the creases of his jeans and sleeves behind knee and elbow also became marked with sweat like dark-blue ink.

"It's not *that* hot," said the driver. Eventually, after a silence, he suggested to himself: "Perhaps he's scared. Maybe."

Eventually the bright canary taxi turned down the High Street and sped towards the ocean. The black Mercedes followed it down to the docks.

In procession among many other cars they went along the grey dockside, past the sides of ships standing high like battlements in some strange fortification against the South China Sea. At last the taxi stopped, and Feng went aboard one of the tall, dark ships moored in the Telok Ayer Basin. Against orders, one of the agents went onto the ship as soon as Feng came back ashore.

The ship was British. She was called *Wanderer*. In a few days she would leave for Southampton, and she was full of men busily loading her for the voyage. The Company man could find no one to whom Feng had spoken, although one or two remembered having seen him.

Confused, he reported back to base, just in time to find

out that his colleagues in the black Mercedes had finally contrived to lose Feng.

When Lydecker arrived, the situation was explained to him. Lydecker was tired, dusty, unshaven and very angry indeed. The whole affair, he said, had been unforgivably bungled. Heads would roll if Feng was not found, and he was just the man to wield the axe.

As the ill-tempered day broke into a vivid, catacysmic thunderstorm, Singapore was taken to pieces. Feng was not found. Lydecker, screaming over the electric static of the storm reported to Langley every three hours.

Two fruitless days later, Parmilee recalled him. He, too, as case officer, was extremely unhappy. The whole thing had been too fast and far too shallow for his taste. It had been as though they had been trying to carry water in a sieve. He never got to grips with any of it: this he did not like in the least. It was partly to allay his nebulous feeling of frustration at the indecent brevity of the distant action, and partly just a blind, unreasoning hunch, but on the 4th of July, just before he formally closed the non-action Action, he sent orders to the ship *Lincoln*, apparently innocently moored in Hong Kong, distantly observing the first days of Chinese rule, that she should make all haste for Singapore and shadow the British ship *Wanderer* at extreme range until such time as *Wanderer* should reach her home port of Southampton, for which she had departed two days previously.

Part Two

Action: KALI

Chapter Three

The Ship

Indian Ocean, 17 July 1997

At 1600 hours local time on 17 July 1997, the *Wanderer* was 15 days out of the Singapore Roads, bound for Southampton via the Suez Canal.

She had taken a slow course against the currents and recent monsoon up the Straits of Malacca, through the Nicobar Islands, in a great arc south of Sri Lanka and India, then through the Maldive Islands and along the Carlsberg Ridge, and finally north-west towards Socotra and the Red Sea.

At 15 seconds past 1600 the bomb in the engine room exploded.

Wanderer had been built in the late sixties by Harland & Wolff in Belfast. She had been designed as an old-fashioned, three-castle ocean-going cargo vessel, a throwback to the pre-container days; and her prime function was still to carry goods between England and the Far East. In the late eighties however, J.J. Hyde & Co., the owners of the South Indian Line, had bought her, had her extensively refitted though not really modernized, and added five expensive staterooms to her high superstructure. These were mainly for the directors of the company, but were also available to other people when not in use by them. The fine profit

Wanderer returned, however, came mainly from the heavy goods she carried below in her holds.

When the bomb in the engine room blew up, the great engines raced wildly and then stopped forever, causing *Wanderer* to lurch abruptly to port. In No 1 hold, 500 tons of Japanese iron girders, loaded in the Singapore entrepôt, broke free from the chains which held them in place and tore through the hull, and so the bomb, which would otherwise have simply disabled her, caused the ship to begin to sink. A gaping hole opened 20 ft aft of the bow on the starboard and less than two fathoms under the agitated surface of the ocean as the girders spilt out into the water, tumbling end over end through the ruined plates like giant matches escaping from a ruined matchbox. It took a little over 12 seconds for No 1 hold to flood. Someone in Singapore had neglected to fasten the watertight bulkhead door which divided it from No 2 hold. It took longer for No 2 hold, packed tight with Indian rice, to flood, but not much.

Aft of No 2 was the engine room itself, beneath the old-fashioned midships bridge house. The explosion here, with its epicentre by the massive engines, had been of sufficient force to damage a few plates, but Chief Engineer O'Rorke, together with two GP seamen who had escaped the full force of the blast, managed to staunch the small seepage of water. In their shocked state, and because of their concern with the buckled plates, none of them noticed that the explosion had also damaged the forward watertight door which separated them from No 2 hold. Two minutes after No 2 had flooded, with the saturated rice already swelling with that inevitable vegetable strength which allows grass stems to split flagstones, some two minutes and 45 seconds after the explosion, Chief Engineer O'Rorke looked up from what he was doing, and saw several fine jets of water spraying out round the edge of the damaged door, and began to yell,

26

"Look out!" Before he had even opened his mouth properly, the door gave way. It exploded inwards, bolts and hinges sheered by the weight of the water behind it. It hit O'Rorke in the chest, swept his body down the whole length of the engine room and crushed it against the after wall. The two seamen panicked and tried to walk through the soggy flood of water and rice to reach the ladder up out of the engine room. Neither of them made it.

By 1605, local time No 1 and No 2 holds, and the engine room were completely flooded. Chief Engineer O'Rorke, two Engineers, and twelve GP seamen were dead; but the *Wanderer*'s rate of sinking was slowing down. It might have taken her another hour to vanish beneath the Indian Ocean, but at 1607 the boilers blew up, and after that it was only a matter of minutes.

At 1530 precisely Alec Stone came into the bar. Stone was a broad, solid man approaching early middle age slowly and easily. He had broad shoulders and the deep chest of a rugby forward. Later, perhaps, he would run to fat, but at the moment he wore his solid muscles with an air of suppressed power. He moved with quiet confidence and an almost feminine precision, as though he was always aware of what he was doing – even in the smallest particular – and how he was doing it. He entered the bar and made his way silently to a table, sat down and raised his left hand a few inches above the polished teak to summon the bar steward. As he approached, Stone took an old gunmetal cigarette case and a silver cigarette lighter out of the breast pocket of his short-sleeved shirt, opened the case with a practised flick of his finger, took out a long low-tar cigarette, and lit it. "Whisky please," he said to the bar steward, in a puff of smoke.

27

The steward moved away silently thinking it had been a waste of time even asking: every day since Singapore Mr Stone had come into the bar at 1130 and stayed until lunchtime; he had come in again at 1530 and stayed until tea; he had returned finally at 2230 and stayed until after midnight. And he always drank whisky.

Stone looked at the silver lighter before he put it back in his pocket. Inscribed on it were the words 'To Alec From Anne With Love'. Anne had been his wife. When she found out the truth about him she had left him and gone home to her mother's house in Belfast. She had been blown up by an IRA bomb soon afterwards. Years ago now, and it hurt more than ever. He leaned back in his chair, cleared his mind of sadness with a conscious effort, and extended his feet. The blue smoke from his cigarette curled lethargically above his head and climbed slowly the still, hot air until the air conditioning fussily swept it away. Stone stared out of the window. If he closed his eyes until the lashes almost met, he could cut out sufficient glare to see the faint line of the horizon where the painfully bright blue-white of the sky met the equally painful green-white of the sea. He drew on his cigarette again and let the smoke out in a long, carefully controlled breath as though smoking were some sort of arcane yoga exercise. According to the old-fashioned thermometer on the wall outside the bar door, the shade temperature was 120°F. Stone longed for England, home and coolness more with each drop of sweat which trickled down his torso.

The bar steward brought the whisky at 1535.

Stone continued to look out of the window until his eyes began to water, then he shook his head, slightly angry with himself. It was childish, always testing himself – and yet he seemed to do it automatically now, like a wrestler thoughtlessly squeezing a rubber ball to strengthen his forearm while doing other things. He was always exploring the boundaries of his capability – always finding out how long he could look at the sun. He reached his long hand out absently and picked up his drink. The ice chimed against the glass; Stone's hand was shaking. He looked at it for a moment with a detached air, then lifted the glass to his mouth with his usual self-aware gesture. He looked around the bar, suddenly, as though he had just heard a sound, but there was nobody there. He drew on his cigarette again and glanced at his watch: nearly a quarter to four.

None of this interrupted Stone's train of thought. Even the regular habits and steady drinking which had filled the last two weeks had been another such game: he had never before studied himself under conditions of opulent routine, where the greatest danger came from ice injudiciously swallowed, and the greatest failure would be to get falling-down drunk. The temptation was to get drunk as quickly as possible and to stay that way until Southampton. But instead, he worked to a simple, unvarying routine – getting as near drunk as he could manage while still being sober, four times a day.

Just before 1600, Mrs Gash bustled into the bar, calling, "Letty? Letty?" in her strident Bronx voice. Stone nodded at her with his usual absent half-smile. Mrs Gash went "Yoo-Hoo!" and waved at him. Stone nodded again. Mrs Gash started to walk towards him, slipping off the ermine stole which, even in this heat, habitually adorned her doughy shoulders. But just as she did so, Miss Buhl – Letty – answered her call with all the careful promptness of an English professional travelling companion. Mrs Gash turned to talk to her. Stone went back to his whisky. He liked Mrs Gash enormously: her broad vivaciousness and studied vulgarity charmed and amused him.

From the moment she saw his dark, brooding profile, she had been asking Stone to do a turn. She had seen his

29

Hamlet some years ago at Stratford. He might have obliged her, had Eldridge Gant not been aboard. To do any acting in front of Gant would be the equivalent of a carthorse racing a thoroughbred. He might just as well have taken on Branagh, Olivier or Burton.

Stone finished his whisky, brooding darkly over his lack of true genius, and signalled the bar steward for another. Then he crushed his cigarette which had burned down to the filter. Mrs Gash and Miss Buhl sat in the corner by the door, looking like a frog talking to a sparrow. The bar steward came over with Stone's drink and placed it carefully on the table. Stone nodded his thanks. The steward turned and began to walk back to the bar. Then the floor seemed to rise in a brief blister. Stone's whisky jumped into the air and then settled back with a small, distinct, click. The windows vanished outwards in a hail of deadly shards. Mrs Gash was thrown back against the wall. Miss Buhl was thrown to the floor. Stone was lifted out of his seat. His shins crashed painfully against the table. His chair toppled over but his body, rolling with the shock, automatically saved him from greater injury.

The bar steward took off. His tray flew one way, his neatly-folded cloth another. His body curled in mid-air until his knees were pushed against his chest. His head snapped back and then forward so that his body followed, seeming to dive head-first into the bar. His neck caught the sharp, brass-bound outer edge, his full weight pivoting on the first two vertebrae of his spinal column. There was an audible crack and his arms and legs shot out, widespread and rigid. His body cartwheeled over the bar to smash into the bottle-racks on the wall.

Stone never really heard the explosion. There were a few moments of darkness and he suddenly found himself sitting on the floor, bruised and dazed. Glass was tumbling off the bottle racks behind the bar. Mrs Gash was swearing colourfully, and Miss Buhl tutting somewhere behind him. he knew with a certainty born of experience that the bar steward was dead.

The only thing he couldn't work out was why, on a perfectly steady table, set solidly on the floor, his whisky glass should start to slide away leaving a trail of whisky to glisten in the suffocating sunshine and dry instantly like the track of a giant snail on the bright polished wood.

At 1600 Eldridge Gant glanced up from the pages of Eugene O'Neill's classic drama *Long Day's Journey into Night*. His eye caught the clockface above the door in his stateroom and he thought, "1600". Then he smiled. He hadn't thought in military time since 'Nam and yet he had caught himself doing it more frequently of late – perhaps because he was on board ship, perhaps because of the interview he had given to the *Straits Times* in Singapore which had brought back so many memories.

All this thought was fleeting. He glanced back down at O'Neill's deathless words even before the red second hand jumped on. Not only was *Long Day's Journey into Night* Gant's favourite play, but he had also agreed to take the part of James Tyrone on Broadway later in the year, with the promise of a transfer of the whole production to the West End of London after an extended run in New York. He had decided to come back from Singapore by sea in order to give himself a rest, he had told the *Straits Times* reporter – among so many other things – and to give himself a chance to get out of the consumingly powerful character of his Macbeth which had taken the Far East by storm over the last few months. But he was looking forward to London especially, and outdoing even Olivier's legendary

James Tyrone – perhaps even doing it at the Barbican if the Royal Shakespeare Company would let him.

As a younger man, Eldridge Gant had been hailed as the new Orson Welles of the American cinema, but the Viet Nam War had put an end to that. He had joined the Army, much against everyone's wishes, and for four years he had seemingly disappeared into the ranks. In fact, he had joined the Special Forces and spent two years shuttling back and forth between the John F Kennedy Center and various war zones as part of the advisory service called the Military Assistance Training Advisor Department, but universally known from its initial capital letters as 'Mill around 'til ambushed'.

He never discussed what he did and rarely even thought about it. When he came out, his life in the cinema was over for two reasons.

First, he was no longer bankable. Secondly, he discovered within himself the need for a live audience – the fear, the excitement, 'the roar of the greasepaint the smell of the crowd' as Wilde or Barnum had put it. He had set about rebuilding his career, therefore, exclusively on stage, and nowadays he transcended comparison even with Barrymore. He was in fact the American Olivier that *Time* magazine had called him: the greatest actor of his age and generation, that generation being too old for comparison with Branagh and the young Turks of the Brat Pack. He was a household name in four continents – although he was rarely glimpsed even on television – and had the almost totally unrestricted entrée of the truly great into almost every country in the world. The President had hinted when last they met that if the policy of detente continued to flourish, then Gant could pick his own company and take any great play he wished to be performed in Beijing itself.

Gant was tall, bony but not thin. He had a mobile, expressive face and large, long hands seemingly made for gesture. When he was at rest, or when concentrating, as now, Gant seemed almost featureless. He was handsome in a conventional way – lacking the classic profile of Redford, Gere or Brosnan or even Alec Stone – and his face did not gain any memorable power until it was animated by some strong emotion, real or (as was more usual) assumed. Eldridge Gant in the flesh left an impression only of height – he was as tall as Eastwood and Heston – and of white hair and of indefinable power.

Now, at 1600 Gant was totally at peace. Only his restless eyes and hands betrayed his total absorption in O'Neill's words as he turned the pages of his priceless signed First Edition of the play, one of the more expensive gifts among the many left in the Purser's office by his legion of admirers before the *Wanderer* sailed.

When the bomb in the engine room exploded Gant hit the floor, rolled into the corner beside his bunk and came up onto his feet in one swift motion. Then he was thrown onto the bunk itself as the ship lurched first one way and then the other. When the movement stopped he came off the bunk at a dead run, yanked the door of his stateroom open and swung into the passage. There, he found the Purser, whose face and starched jacket were exactly the same colour, leaning up against the wall. "What's going on?" he asked.

"I don't know, sir. I think we may have hit something. I'm sure it's nothing to worry about. I'll just go and see." The Purser staggered off and Gant stood for a moment deciding what to do. He knew nothing about ships but this felt fairly serious to him. He went back into his stateroom and began to search quickly but methodically through his baggage. In a matter of moments he noticed that the floor was beginning to tilt and he began to work faster. He had been sitting reading in his shirt sleeves. Now he tore the shirt off completely. Around his still trim waist he buckled a black waterproof moneybelt, then he emptied the contents of his briefcase onto his bed and began to sort through the jumbled pile of papers and books. The first thing he slid into safety was the play he had just been reading.

When Gant came out into the passageway five minutes later he had changed his casual trousers for a pair of heavy jeans. He had put on a light but substantial roll-neck sweater which he wore untucked so that it came down past his waist concealing the slight bulge there. He had Reebok trainers on his feet and for the first time in many years he wore no socks. Under his right arm he carried a lifebelt and a sunhat. In his left hand he carried a pair of sunglasses. He had tried to be as practical as possible but what he knew of shipwreck he had gleaned largely from the pages of *Pericles* and *The Tempest*. That this was a shipwreck he had no doubt and the knowledge transformed him. The indolent reader of *Long Day's Journey* was gone. Eldridge Gant was enjoying himself.

When Gant arrived in the corridor the high walls and narrow floor emphasized just how steeply the ship was now angled. He put on his hat and sunglasses, and glanced at his watch. Only some six minutes had passed since the explosion – extraordinary! It felt so much longer. He knocked on the door of the stateroom opposite his own. There was no reply so he put his head round the door and called, "Rebecca? Are you there?" There was silence, so he glanced around the room and went out. He quickly jogged to the companionway. He glanced at his watch again – 1607 – sprang easily up the stairs and walked onto the after-deck.

Standing just by the companionway door, under the shadow behind the bridge, Gant surveyed the bustle before him. All along the port side the lifeboats had been swung out on their davits and the crew was lowering them into the

Thank you for supporting the Red Cross.

Please use this bookmark to inspire others to support the life-saving work of the British Red Cross.

Are you ready for winter?

Take a few simple steps to be better prepared for severe weather. Visit redcross.org.uk/readyforwinter to find out how.

'The Snowman™ and The Snowdog' © used with kind permission of Snowdog Enterprises Ltd 2017

recycle

Supporting

BritishRedCross

44 Moorfields
London EC2Y 9AL
0300 456 11 55
redcross.org.uk

The British Red Cross Society, incorporated by Royal Charter 1908, is a charity registered in England and Wales (220949) and Scotland (SC037738) and Isle of Man (0752).

WDD17 B2

Season's
Greetings

still-distant water. Gant immediately took a step forward and trod in a small pool of water. His foot slipped, and, trying not to fall forward up the slope of the deck reaching like a gentle hillside to the high poop deck, he staggered back through the door behind him. As he did so there was a terrible roar and the whole deck reared up like a wood and iron tidal wave.

Such was the force of the explosion that Gant was hurled bodily backwards. He would have gone to his death down the companionway but his life jacket, held firmly in his right hand now, caught on the top of the bannister and brought him down winded but safe on the steps. The power of the blast slammed the door above him and as the *Wanderer* rolled over and over towards port, Gant rolled too, stunned and in the dark.

After some time the ship righted herself, saved for the moment by the weight of rice and water in her holds. Gant struggled to his feet and pulled himself back up to the door. There was a great spear of 2 × 4 timber through it now but Gant managed to open it and get out. He stepped through it automatically, still a little dazed, and felt his foot slipping. He looked down and there was nothing there. Wildly he flung his hand back and caught the doorpost. Then he stood for a moment on one foot balanced precariously on 18 in of broken planking as he tried to comprehend what had happened to the deck.

Where a few moments earlier there had been perhaps 50 men busily swinging out lifeboats now there was no one. The ship's rails were twisted but unbroken and there was nobody standing beside them. What was left of the lifeboats hung smashed to pieces on buckled davits but all the men were gone. Gant closed his eyes for a moment, revelling in the sudden darkness after the terrible brightness of the day, and then opened them again to make sure. But there was no mistake. They were all gone. And where the deck itself had been there was now the nothingness into which Gant had so nearly stepped. Roughly circular, curving away from his precarious perch and out nearly to the sides of the ship, then closing to meet under the overhang of the poop, were the edges of a ragged hole. These were turned upwards like the edges of a bomb crater and with each sluggish movement of the ship some board or piece of planking would topple into the abyss, banging and clattering on its way down – always landing with a distant splash.

Gant looked down into the shadows. A bright beam of sunlight revealed a maelstrom of foam which even as he watched began to creep up the inside of the ship. Irrationally then he yelled into the hole, "Is there anybody there?"

At 1600 Silas Wells was sound asleep in his bunk in Stateroom 5. He had had a long session the night before in the bar with Alec Stone. Among other things in a so-far fairly active life Wells had once been a reporter and his nose told him there was a story to be had about the quiet Englishman. It was certainly worth prying into – especially after the rumours which had been flying around Singapore about him before he was summarily slung out on his ear. But even if there was nothing interesting after all, he would still have a nice exclusive about Eldridge Gant and the nubile Miss Rebecca Dark. So it had been a hard night, keeping pace with Stone through two bottles of Tomintoul Glenlivet single malt whisky while plying him subtly with questions about his past and present employment – apart of course from the months he had just spent as Oberon in the Travelling Theatre's production of *A Midsummer Night's Dream*.

When Stone had finally clammed up Wells had turned

to watch the tall white-haired man and the tall black-haired girl for a moment. When he turned back Stone had gone. Wells' eyes had narrowed and the corners of his mouth turned down – he hadn't even heard him go.

He didn't hear the explosion in the engine room either, but suddenly his slight, skinny body was dumped on the floor and he sprang awake. Automatically he looked at his watch – just gone four: he'd been asleep for nearly 12 hours. He swept his long blond hair out of his eyes and sat up. At first he thought it was the hangover but then it suddenly became quite clear that the floor actually was at an angle. Like Gant and Stone, Wells didn't know much about ships but he knew enough to get his clothes on as quickly as possible. Then, also like Gant, he started strapping things under his shirt.

Because he had been so deeply asleep he was slower about it than Gant and he was just stepping out of his stateroom door as the actor was stepping onto the aft deck. Wells turned the other way, however, and began to run up the forward steps. Halfway up he met Bates, the radio operator, coming down. "Seen the Captain, sir?"

"Sorry. Important?"

"Weather. We're in for a bit of a blow . . ." And then the boilers blew up. Wells, thrown forward, hit Bates in the lower stomach as though he had been performing a rugby tackle. Bates folded forward over his shoulder and they tumbled down the companionway together. "What the hell was that?" asked Wells when he had regained his breath.

"I was on a steamer once, maybe 20 years ago and I heard a sound like that," said Bates dreamily. "It was the boilers going up."

"God save us! What'll we do?"

"Better get to my radio."

37

"Send for help?"

"Well, radio our position: the old girl's beyond help now."

The radio shack was behind the bridge, a wooden excrescence reaching out onto the deck. When they got to the door which had saved the life of Eldridge Gant, Bates noticed the 2 × 4 wooden beam through it. Tacked to one side of the beam was a black wire. The two men stood briefly in the doorway, shocked into disbelief, then Bates gestured to the wire on the 2 × 4. "That's about all that's left of the radio now," he said, then suddenly he was retching, doubled forward. Wells only just caught him in time to stop him falling into the cavernous hole, and as he pulled him back into the safety of the companionway he heard echoing faintly from beneath his feet a voice crying, "Yes, here. Oh here! Help, please! Here!" He sat Bates on the steps. "Are you OK?" he said.

"Yes. It was just that thump you gave me in the guts. Did I hear someone yelling down that hole?"

"Yes."

"Who was it?"

"I don't know, Bates. You wait here while I go and find out."

Bates nodded and leaned against the bannister. Wells went down one side of the corridor knocking on the stateroom doors, and back up the other to where he had started. At this end of the corridor the wall bulged slightly but Wells did not notice. He knocked on the last door – Stateroom 2. "Yes, oh yes!" came a voice. Wells thought: Rebecca Dark, and opened the door.

And suddenly, like Gant on the deck far above, Wells was swinging over nothing. Where the state-room had been there was now a hole that went down to the pale oily maelstrom of the sea far below. Nothing was left except, where the other side of the state-room had been, a square of floor in the corner jutted over the abyss. Bolted to it was half a bunk, and on this, naked, on the far side, sat Rebecca Dark.

At 1600 Rebecca Dark turned on the shower in Stateroom 2 and slipped her long body out of her red silk robe. She had put her hair up in a careless knot and jammed a green plastic shower cap over it. Rebecca moved with a grace that was totally unselfconscious – markedly different from the controlled movements of Alec Stone or her employer Eldridge Gant. It was not that she was unaware of the beauty of her fine legs, or the way the supple slimness of her waist emphasised the downward curve of hips and the upward rise of breasts; indeed she ate with a certain degree of care to ensure that these things remained so for as long as possible; but – having a fine figure and doing what was necessary to maintain it – she did not let it rule her. She had much the same relationship with the black waves of her hair and her fine-boned face: not that she had ever actually stopped and thought about herself for long enough to work out these things in detail. However, the results of all this thoughtless, semi-automatic care rarely failed to turn heads and occasionally to elicit wolf-whistles from the trenchantly genderist.

Rebecca had worked for Eldridge Gant for nearly a year now as secretary and general assistant. She and Gant had an easy relationship somewhat along the lines of uncle and niece. Certainly, in all the time she had known him he had never been anything warmer than distantly avuncular. Indeed she always felt that he was working to maintain a distance between them which safeguarded the sacrosanct areas of privacy – both mental and physical – with which he liked to surround himself. For example, during at least one night in every city they visited he would insist on going off Heaven knew where on his own. Rebecca had once enquired about these jaunts – she would not do so again.

Further, the respect to which she felt he was due as her employer served to hide the fact that she must never get too close to him without him knowing: she must always knock on his door and must never enter without his permission – no matter what. As far as she was concerned it was only common courtesy but he saw it as something more. He had explained it to her once and she could see his point. The fact was, he said, that when one led such a public life as his, privacy even in the smallest things became of paramount importance. So they remained on slightly distant terms and each was quite content with the arrangement. Gant had an efficient secretary who never impinged needlessly on his privacy and whom, incidentally, it was a pleasure to be seen with; Rebecca had a job which she enjoyed and performed well and she also got to see the world – First Class.

As Rebecca stood beneath the shower and began absent-mindedly to soap the flat brown precipice of her stomach her mind was somewhat removed from her employer. Last night in the bar Mr Wells – "Call me Silas, sweetie" – had been watching her very closely. She rather thought the interesting, silent Mr Stone had given him the brush-off. That Wells is really rather detestable, she thought. And as she did so, a giant hand seemed to lift her and slam her against the shower wall. Winded, she began to slip. Then the wall of the solid little cubicle hit her in the back and as she fell forward again the iron tap smashed against her head just above the hairline. As she collapsed the rose burst off the shower and a cloud of superheated steam roared over her to blast a hole in the heavy-duty plastic of the stall. One or two drops fell on her lower back and buttocks but she was already unconscious.

In fact it was this steam, which would have killed her had she still been standing up, that saved her life. Under normal circumstances the blow to her head would have laid her out for more than ten minutes but the scalding water dripping onto her hurt sufficiently to cut through the darkness in her head a little under five minutes after the first explosion. At first, aware only of the pain in her back, she thought she had damaged her spine but when she looked over her shoulder the red spots astride the brown-white line left by her bikini bottom showed what had really happened. She pulled herself to her feet and staggered a little on the slope of the deck.

Her first thought was for Gant as his had been for her – she had been unconscious when he called to her – and she ran into her stateroom to get her clothes. As she was still rather groggy she sat on her bunk in order to pull on her panties, then as the effort started her head aching she lay back to catch her breath.

As she did so, the floor of her cabin vanished through the roof. A tremendous wrench slapped her head against her pillow with stunning force. Her hands automatically clutched, slipped, clutched again. She was clinging for life. Clinging literally, for she found herself on the top half of a bed hanging over a cavern whose further reaches she could not see, and the bed, like the cave, was tilting farther and farther to port trying to hurl her off her perch. She worked her hand down the small space between the remains of the bedhead and the wall, closed her eyes and hung on as the ship tilted over.

Just when Rebecca became certain that she could hold on no longer, the movement ceased and then reversed. Moments after, Rebecca was sitting on her ledge safe for the moment and sound. Then she heard the voice of Eldridge Gant call faintly from the great cauldron of brightness above her head, "Is there anybody there?"

"Yes!" she screamed, but the word came out in a broken whisper. She cleared her throat desperately and called again but the slow clatter of a falling plank like a single drum at a funeral drowned out her second cry. A little later she thought she saw two figures outlined against the white-hot disk of the sky. She was still calling to Gant, "Yes, here! Oh, here! Help, please, here!" Then they too were gone.

The seconds crept by, each punctuated by the falling of more timber. She followed one bright plank with her eyes as it fell end over end through the ragged hole where this deck had been, through the metal-toothed void where the next deck down had been, and so on deeper and deeper into the black-shadowed pit until the white-foamed madness of the water below engulfed it and sucked it down. Then above the roar she heard a knocking at her door and called out. The door opened, and there, as though framed in a picture high on a huge wall, stood Silas Wells. Wells' unbelieving eyes probed the darkness and finally rested upon Rebecca. It was then she realized that she was in fact very nearly in the condition he leeringly reduced her to in his mind every time they met. Automatically her legs crossed over her flimsy panties and her free hand crept up to cover the coral tips of her breasts.

"Creeping Jesus!" said Wells. Rebecca said nothing.

Then Wells was gone without another word and Rebecca began to pray. For perhaps two minutes she sat there with tears streaming silently down her face as the forward tilt on the ship became more and more noticeable. But Wells had only gone for help and suddenly the door slammed open again.

A little way down the passage he had found a hosepipe

and an axe in a box on the wall labelled 'In case of fire break glass.' Wells had broken the glass. Now he stood in the doorway swinging the heavy brass nozzle of the flat canvas hose. The first time he threw it he missed but the second time it landed on the bed and Rebecca held it with fierce concentration, far more worried about survival than about modesty.

"Push it under the leg of the bed, take in the slack and throw it back!" yelled Wells. She did so, though it was hard to do one-handed. The first try reached him by something of a miracle. Wells pulled as much off the wall as he could and cut it with the axe. Then he chopped the nozzle off the hose. Taking the two cut ends he passed them through the railings at the bottom of the stairway and tied them together.

Rebecca had worked out what to do next and was already busy when he staggered back to the doorway and called "Tie yourself a sling." She pulled her hand out from behind the bed, took a loop of the flat white canvas and tied a double knot in it. She slipped the loop over her head and sat, precariously balanced, waiting. Wells tightened the big loop by re-tying the knot at his end and then tested by pulling with all his strength. It was OK.

"Sit on the very edge," he yelled. Gingerly, she did so. "Now lean forward. Farther!" Rebecca obeyed. Shockingly close, the wild-foam of white water boiling in through the ruptured bottom beneath the engine room waited to claim her. She closed her eyes, kicked forward and fell off the ledge. "Hold on!" yelled Wells, needlessly. The hose tightened with a jerk. The sling of rough canvas scraped up her ribs before catching under her arms. The top of the big loop sprang taut between the foot of the bannister and the head of the bed as she swung above the submerged ruin of the engine room.

There was a loud crack from behind her and the bed began to tip. Wells pulled frantically at his end of the makeshift breeches-buoy. The knot he had tied slid past his shoulder and out over the dizzy drop. Turning in slow circles Rebecca was pulled inch by inch towards safety. She was two-thirds of the way over when the leg of the bed broke. Wells saw it go and in that second before the full weight came onto his arms he managed to take a few steps backwards. Rebecca was also thinking with a speed born of desperation. As the whole of her ledge tumbled noisily into the water behind and below her, she grabbed the far side of the loop. Then Wells was staggering forward and Rebecca was swinging 15 ft and more below, where C Deck used to be. The rest of the loop which had spanned the stateroom swung beneath her tapping the razor edges of twisted steel and dragging in the water.

"Bates!" yelled Wells and abruptly there was another man helping to pull her up.

Within a few moments they were helping her through the doorframe and into the corridor. Bates swung his white uniform jacket over her shoulders and they supported her out onto the unbearable brightness of the forward deck, and it was not until then that she thought of the show she must have given Wells. But somehow she thought now that he probably hadn't been looking too closely after all.

There was a small group of people there. "Rebecca," said Gant stepping towards her. He looked faintly ridiculous in his sunhat but there was a great deal of relief in his voice. Mrs Gash and Letty Buhl were there with him and Alec Stone lying on the deck with blood on his forehead.

"What happened?" asked Wells, relinquishing Rebecca into her employer's charge and gesturing towards Stone.

"Miss Buhl nearly went over the side when the second explosion happened," said Gant. "Stone saved her. When

I got there he was lying on his belly hanging onto her. She was dangling over the side. He was out cold but he simply wouldn't let go." There was awe in his voice.

Then Bates said, "Where's the lifeboat?" Nobody answered. The green jaws of the ocean closed over the high forecastle with a roar like a waterfall.

"Here, Slobowski, what's the time?" yelled Slattery.

"Nearly sixteen-hundred."

"Jeez! You'd think it would get cooler this time in the day." The big Irish American turned back to his work.

"Out here?" answered Slobowski, the square Pole from Chicago, "It never gets cool while the sun's up."

"At noit now," chimed in little weasely Dublin O'Keefe with a corny whining brogue, "At noit now it's a different matter entirely so it is. You Americans have it all too easy, you know? All that air-conditioning's made you soft. Terrible. Terrible. Day's too hot. Night's too cold."

"Shut up O'Keefe and do a bit of work," said young Mr Spooner the 20-year-old Third Officer who was still wet behind the ears. They were a unique little group among the Chinese and Malay crew. But they were also much more troublesome than the accommodating orientals, so today they were swabbing the deck.

"Yes sir!" said O'Keefe. "Yes sir, indeedy sir. Mr Laughton, could I ever be troubling for a little of your water? His Majesty here . . ."

When the engine room blew up they were all thrown onto the deck and Laughton's bucket toppled over sending a small tidal wave of cold soapy water over O'Keefe as *Wanderer* slewed first one way and then the other. The men began to pick themselves up. By the time they were all together it was obvious she was going down by the head. Young

45

Spooner turned, a little at a loss. "Better start swinging the lifeboats out," he said.

"Oh sir, come off it, sir," whined O'Keefe. "There's no rush. 'Abandon ship' hasn't even been sounded yet, sir. Let us go and change sir. We're all wet." The others were in agreement with him for once. They all had personal effects they wanted to get if they were going to abandon.

Spooner was very young. He wavered. O'Keefe took the lack of a blank refusal as permission and started for the aftercastle where their accommodation was. Spooner let it slide and after a while he followed the men. The crew's quarters in the high poop were cramped but not uncomfortable. Here, the Europeans had a little, segregated, room of their own. Spooner and the men crowded in and the deckhands started to strip off their clothes and put on dry ones. Then one after another they turned to some private corner and began to secrete bundles and packages under their shirts. "Come along now, hurry up, please," said Spooner, concerned that while there had been no signal to abandon ship a purposeful group of Chinese crewmen had arrived on the deck below under the command of Willy Windle, the Second Officer and were swinging out lifeboats. Where was the Captain? he wondered.

The Captain and First Officer were at that moment trying to ascertain the extent of the damage below and were just beside the engine room.

"Hurry up," repeated Spooner anxiously.

"Aw sir, just a minute, sir," whined O'Keefe, smirking round his unresponsive shipmates.

"Shut up, O'Keefe," snapped Spooner, ill-tempered. His own whites were beginning to dry uncomfortably on him. He would be a mass of prickly heat tonight, he thought. He turned to the door saying, "Come on then," and he noticed two things: almost the whole crew was on the after deck

46

swinging out the lifeboats; Mr Gant in a white hat clutching a bright orange life jacket was tumbling backwards through a dark doorway behind the bridge. He must have slipped, thought Spooner.

Then the deck took off and soared in a million jagged fragments into the air. It was like watching a flock of starlings take flight. Or like black fireworks, thought Spooner distantly, totally overwhelmed by the great roaring. The last thing he saw before falling backwards was Second Officer Windle flying impossibly high in the air, a man, at first quite recognisable, then a shape, then a cross among many crosses then, suddenly and for no apparent reason, five separate pieces which began to fall with the rest towards the sea. Spooner fell onto his back and rolled as the ship rolled. "Sweet Mary Mother of God," said O'Keefe. They all lay stunned as the *Wanderer* heeled over.

It was Laughton, the huge, quiet ex-boxer from Liverpool who took charge. Spooner had knocked himself out as he fell. Blood trickled down his forehead. "Better get to a boat," he said.

"Over that?" screamed O'Keefe, waving at the yawning crater in the deck.

"There's one on the poop," said Slobowski, the Pole from Chicago. "It's a cutter more than a proper lifeboat, but I guess it'll do." They piled up tables and chairs until Slattery could climb up and smash the skylight. The big Bronx Irishman pulled them all up through, one at a time after him onto the sloping poop. Laughton went last, handing up Third Officer Spooner's inert body to Slobowski and Slattery. When he got up he saw that the others were pulling the old green canvas cover from the long cutter and preparing to swing it out.

"Better hurry," said Laughton. The angle of the deck was

increasing as she went down by the head. The propellors and rudder were nearly clear of the water.

"We'll never get it down past the rudder," whined O'Keefe, but even as he said it the great fin of metal toppled flat onto its side with a sound like a massive gong being struck. They began to winch the boat down as quickly as they could, so that it slid off the dripping rudder clear of the blades and into the water. Laughton slung Spooner over one massive shoulder and climbed down the gantry rope. The rest followed as best they could.

Once in the boat they unshipped the oars and were just about to row away when Laughton said, "Once round the ship. There may be more alive and all the other boats are gone."

"They're all dead," said O'Keefe belligerently. "Let's just get the hell out of here."

"Sorry," said Laughton gently, "no can do." His baby-blue eyes wandered over the rest of the men in the lifeboat, half expecting them to back O'Keefe and get away to safety but Slattery shrugged his massive shoulders, grinning his Irish grin and Slobowski the Pole nodded once. So they rowed down the side of the sinking ship yelling, "Is there anybody there?"

"Yes, here!" cried Eldridge Gant the actor, suddenly appearing just forward of the bridge in a white sunhat which made him look faintly ridiculous.

"Jump!" yelled O'Keefe, eager to be away.

"GET OFF OF THERE!" shouted Slobowski.

"DO IT NOW MAN!" Laughton yelled.

"But there are several more . . . let's see . . . seven of us all together . . ."

"Jesus Christ," muttered O'Keefe.

"GET THEM ALL OFF. QUICKLY," bellowed Laughton, concerned now that by the time seven people could sort themselves out and get to the boat they would all be sucked down after the *Wanderer* and drown.

"DO IT NOW MAN!" Laughton repeated, gripping the tiller so tightly the dry wood began to crack. Unconscious still beside Laughton's corded thigh, Spooner stirred a little. Five passengers and the radio operator crowded to the side of the ship, paused, then four of them jumped. The men in the boat rowed as near as they dared and quickly dragged them aboard: Letty Buhl and Mrs Gash, Rebecca, and Wells. Grant and Bates followed with the unconscious Alec Stone, held between them. They supported him to the boat and climbed in after he had been pulled aboard.

"Now row!" yelled Laughton and they rowed for dear life. Behind them the *Wanderer* slid faster and faster under the water. Waves swept restlessly up the foredeck and crashed against the mid-deck bridge. With the ease of a stiletto, the ship plunged into the bosom of the Indian Ocean. White spume reached up like fingers grasping the funnel. The waves met other waves cascading out of the great hole amidships.

With all of the crewmen slick with sweat at the oars, gasping under the furnace heat of the afternoon sun and the passengers lying in the bilge all nearly as helpless as Alec Stone, they took the lifeboat through the water in great lurches of effort away from the stricken ship. The angry waves roared around the poop, driving the last of the air out of cabins and passageways in great roars and belches and screams of sound. A mountain of froth spewed upwards whipped by the force of the water out of the bowels of the drowned steel shell. And she was gone.

But in going she had torn a great hole in the ocean and the water rushed to fill it in a quietly hissing and infinitely ominous whirlpool. And the lifeboat began to move with it sliding back down the liquid slope.

49

"Row!" yelled Laughton, his voice breaking with the strain. But their effort faltered and ultimately they sat in stunned silence as their tiny craft was swept in a rocking spiral back towards the madly spinning foam at the centre of the whirlpool. They had gone round three times and were starting on the fourth and last, their boat at a dangerous tilt, when O'Keefe whispered, "It's weakening." And it was.

A few moments later, still caught in the terrible fascination of the thing, they were sitting motionless in the boat, spinning round and round like a mad compass needle in the middle of the Indian Ocean, where the vortex had been, still moved by its power.

They sat long after the boat had stopped moving, sucking the boiling air into their straining lungs. But eventually Slobowski coughed, Stone stirred, O'Keefe's ratty little eyes strayed to the opulent curves of Rebecca Dark's bosom and he rubbed his mouth with the back of his hand. It was 1625, local time.

"I wish I knew what the hell happened," said Laughton.

Chapter Four

The Plans

15 Bowstring Alley, Beijing, 18 July 1997

Feng was watching the wall. It seemed such an ordinary wall, hard and solid-made of grey stone blocks the length of an arm, flaking a little admittedly and not without long lines of rust-coloured moss, but a solid, stable, ordinary wall. Except that every time he took his eyes off it, it would become liquid, vibrate for a moment, begin to sag, and slowly turn into a great drop of stone and trickle onto the floor. It seemed to Feng that it would be a truly beautiful thing to examine this phenomenon, but it never happened when his eyes were fully on it. This was extremely frustrating.

But there was a lot more going on around him so he was not too upset. There was the chair upon which he was sitting, for example. He could not see that, of course, but its surface and curves *felt* so beautiful. The ease of the back, so solidly founded but rising by infinitely slow degrees to the soft ridge supporting his shoulders. The solidity of the seat, so hard, so flat, yet so delicately curved: the length of the legs, surely raising him so high. So very high.

The wall sagged. Feng's eyes snapped back to it: too late. His face pouted like that of a disappointed child. "You're sure you haven't given him too much?" asked the Bee. The doctor shook his head: "No."

51

"What do you see, Feng?" asked the Bee quietly. It was always the first question because he needed to know what sort of a trip Feng was on each time. A really bad trip was useless and could be fatal. He didn't want Feng mad or dead. Not yet. Therefore he asked, "What do you see, Feng?"

Feng said, "Wall." He said it slowly, savouring the shape of the word, examining the movements of chest, throat and mouth which made it. Confident of the totality of the communication.

"What about the wall?" snapped the Bee. He needed to break down Feng's drug-induced self-confidence or he would get nothing but useless one-word answers. He had already had days – weeks – of one-word answers. This was why Feng was on the chair, no longer in the comfortable, ego-bolstering bed. "Wall," said Feng again. The Bee closed his eyes. In spite of his occidental appearance, however, in spite of his jug-handle ears, his fair white skin, his flat broken nose and round blue eyes, he had a truly oriental patience. He was infinitely patient; infinitely painstaking. "What is the wall doing, Feng?" he asked again quietly, calmly. Feng's eyes snapped back to the wall: too late. "Sagging."

"Why is the wall sagging, brother Feng?"

"Watching. Not watching."

"Come now, Feng. You are not being very clear."

"Wall."

"What about the wall?"

"Wall sagging."

"Why?"

"Not watching."

"EXPLAIN!" cried the Bee, hoping to shock Feng out of the senseless round.

It was actually becoming extremely important to Feng

that he should share this unique experience. He made the supreme effort: "Wall is sagging when *not* watching."

"I understand," congratulated the Bee. "That was not so bad, was it?" he soothed. He allowed himself a brief feeling of elation. This was the first half-sensible utterance in ten days. He watched Feng, waiting for a new line of questioning to present itself: one which could be twisted by infinite degrees into a series of questions about the attempted defection – who had he seen? What had he done?

Feng held on to the chair with both hands. "Why are you holding on to the chair brother?"

Feng began to sort out the question into some sort of form. Inside him the chemicals mixed and melded. The nature of the trip subtly began to change. Suddenly he was icy cold. But Feng was preoccupied with the question. The chair, the chair, the chair: "The chair."

"Why are you holding it, brother?"

The chair. Why? Why? Why chair? Why holding? Why holding chair? WHY HOLDING CHAIR: "Fall off."

"Why?" persisted the Bee.

Why? Why fly buy sigh die high my pie try HIGH: "High," ply by cry fry dry pry cry die die die.

"The chair is high?" prompted the voice of God booming from the Heavens.

HIGH die try die DIE: HIGH: SIGH: SILL: WILL: WELL: WALL: WALL! WALL! WALL!

Feng's whole body slewed round. Every muscle and tendon etched clearly beneath his rice-paper skin. Every vein bulged. His eyes started out of his face. The heavy wood chair groaned as its joints strained. The straps binding Feng threatened to snap. The Bee stepped back instantly: "Doctor!" he snapped. The doctor bustled forward but he was far too late.

Feng watched the wall bulge and flow onto the floor

like a massive drop of water. Its edges broke away from the hard edges of reality and it came towards him like a tidal wave. As it hit the floor it gained height. It broke through the roof, its leading edge hollowing until it was a vibrant cliff overhanging him. His body slammed back into the chair, neck straining his head far enough back to see its mountainous crest. High, high, high among the stars he saw a line of white foam. Distantly he heard a roar like the massive jets at Kai Tak and Changi International. The wave was breaking down on him! He just had time to scream before it closed over his head and he drowned.

The Doctor looked up at the Bee, no emotion evident on his bland, round face. "The man is dead," he said. The Bee picked him up and threw him across the room.

The Chinese secret service is called the Social Affairs Department (SAD). It has its headquarters at No 15, Bowstring Alley, Beijing. In the main conference room of this tall old house the Bee reported to his masters a little later. In the discussion that followed, the whole case of the misguided Feng and the action which had grown up around him was examined.

The Chairman himself did not attend the Fourth National Peoples' Conference held between 13 and 17 January that year. However, 2,864 locally elected delegates did, and this mass of excellent party members felt it their duty to streamline their Party. The Party, its mechanics and its civil service. Amongst those whose services were misapplied in political work was Feng. He was moved from a responsible position with the Social Affairs Department itself, to a communal farm near Tsingato. He was a single man, long widowed and childless. He had been accounted effectively childless

54

even before his daughter was killed in Tiannenman Square.

That much was clear. After that, the sequence of events went slightly out of focus. Feng was informed in early June of the decision. He showed no emotion, praised the wisdom of the perspicacious People, and disappeared. He did not go to Tsingato. He did not go anywhere. Apparently he lingered in Beijing briefly, eluding the authorities – who were admittedly overstrained because of the sheer numbers of comrades also streamlined out of their jobs by the wise delegates of the newly Maoist Peoples' Conference.

By the time it became clear that Feng had actually left Beijing, out of control, he was running free. The nature of his work (Second Senior in the Near-Western Section, SAD) made it seem most likely that he would run north into Russia, taking with him some tit-bit of information with which to buy sanctuary. He had been among the brothers seemingly fortunate enough, in the far-off days before the new purity, to have been educated in Moscow. He might therefore have contacts. It was all very feasible. The northern border was closed tight, therefore, while the files in Feng's department were searched. Nothing was missing – but there might, of course, be copies.

Soon it became clear, however, that Feng was not running north, and a new urgency entered the game. The southern borders had not been so carefully patrolled, for what would he want in Hong Kong? Especially as the Colony would revert to the People's Control in a matter of days. Unless, in Moscow during the time of detente he had met agents of another power – America, perhaps, always looking for the main chance.

Lately returned from a delicate mission overseas, the Hummingbird and the Bee were set upon the defector's trail. This pair of agents were used to working outside

55

China, as spies, agents provocateurs, assassins. They were part of a new breed of officer in the SAD. They were people used to taking pro-active action, to moving in those areas traditionally closed to the historically re-active organisation. But nowadays, of course, China was a Tiger of the Pacific Rim – a player upon the world stage. There was a new section to the SAD whose main responsibility was to work overseas, filling the vacuum left by the shortage of the CIA and the FSS as America and Russia discovered what life was like now that the Cold War was a thing of the past. And the Hummingbird and the Bee were the cutting edge of the new, active, department. They were the best.

They tracked Feng south, eating away his two weeks' lead with casual ease. They were close behind when he crossed the New Territories into Hong Kong on the night of 25 June. So close that when the four operatives of CIA Local Station had picked Feng up, the Humming Bird and the Bee had picked up the American agents too. It was a moment's work to dispose of three of them, but unfortunately in the confusion they had lost contact with Feng.

The defector did not know the city. His contact with the CIA had been brief. If they had managed to slip him directions it was unlikely that he would follow them for he would realise that the confusion covering his escape from the two Chinese agents was in fact the epitaph of his protectors.

Even with Check Lap Kok accepting flights, the quickest way out of Hong Kong is Kai Tak airport. They went there immediately just in time to see Feng board a plane for Singapore. With practised ease they disposed of a couple of latecomers, took their tickets and followed Feng onto the plane.

In Singapore they had been unlucky. Last in the queue for baggage check and customs at Changi International they had watched him cross the concourse and saw the two CIA agents pick him up. By the time they had found him again in his bright canary taxi, closely followed by the black Mercedes Benz, he was on his way down to the docks.

They had been deeply disturbed by his visit to the *Wanderer* because they could not work out why he had done it and it was their experience that inconsistency was inevitably sinister. For this reason, when they did eventually get hold of Feng – in the Gentlemen's toilet of a restaurant, where he had stopped to have some tea – the Bee brought him back while the Hummingbird went onto the ship.

At first the plan had seemed to be beautiful in its utter simplicity. Hummingbird would look through the ship and find out who Feng had talked to. But Feng had talked to no one. Furthermore, although there was some coming-and-going, no one resembling an agent went near any place which might serve as a dead letter drop. Feng's information must therefore have remained on board.

The plan changed a little, but became no less beautiful. Hummingbird would remain on board the ship – even should she sail. Feng would be asked to reveal why he had gone aboard. Hummingbird would be told and would act upon the information. But Feng had not broken. The *Wanderer* had sailed with the Hummingbird aboard.

The final plan was even more elegant than the others. Even in the face of Feng's recalcitrance it could be put into effect. The Hummingbird had a small bomb. This would not be used immediately. Sufficient time must pass for the Chinese freighter *Glorious Revolution* to catch up with the British ship. At Hummingbird's discretion, in mid-ocean, the bomb would cripple the *Wanderer*. *Glorious Revolution* would pick up the distress calls and go to her aid. Everyone aboard would be removed. They and the ship would be taken apart.

This last was the most beautiful plan of all: nothing could possibly go wrong.

Chapter Five

The Boat

17–19 July

At first when he woke Stone thought he was blind. All he was aware of was the movement of the boat, an uneven pitching movement which made his stomach reel almost as wildly as his head. He lay without moving, engrossed in the all-consuming endeavour of not being sick. Then, terrifyingly, there washed over him the realisation that he was at the centre of a total absence of light. Sweat ran in a moment all over his body. He felt cold and began to shake.

As a child he had had a recurring nightmare. It always began like this with utter darkness. Soon, he knew, he would find it hard to breathe. Then he would begin to fight against the dark but it would assume substance and become invisible blankets surrounding him, cutting off his air. His struggles would become wilder, using up his small store of oxygen the quicker, wilder and more unavailing and the blindness in his eyes would begin to spread as numbness to his brain and heaviness would hold his arms and legs until the knowledge that he was dying was no longer sufficient motive to make him move as the blankets of the dark bound him tighter and tighter until they became his winding sheet and shroud.

"Mr Stone! Mr Stone, are you awake?" A distant voice, soft and distant. Miss Dark, thought Stone without really being aware of who Miss Dark was. "Mr Stone!" That same voice, more insistent. Stone shook his blind head and it hurt. Unconsciousness was seeping away unnoticed. Stone began to feel external things – hardness under his back, cramp in his legs, the cold: he shivered. "Mr Stone. Alec." The same voice. But Stone was hearing other things now – the mutter of low conversation, the sighing of the restless wind, the irregular lapping of waves on wood beside his head. And he smelt the sea, heavy and salt mixed with something sweeter and more elusive – scent, a woman's scent. He had smelt such scents before, in Paris with Anne. They cost £50 an ounce. He moved his head slightly, exploring the scent. "Anne?" he said.

"Alec?" The quiet voice: not Anne. A slight movement in the corner of his eye. He moved his head. Nothing. "I can't see," said Stone.

"It's dark," said Miss Dark. Miss Dark in the dark.

"I'm not blind, then."

"No. You hit your head."

A vivid flash of memory. He had helped Mrs Gash and Miss Buhl to their feet in the bar after the first explosion. The three of them had gone outside. There was a noticeable list on the ship: she was down by the head. "Come on," he had said, "We'd better go to our muster stations – I don't like the look of this." They had been going down the steps on the front of the bridge towards the forward deck when Mrs Gash had wedged the heel of her shoe in one of the steps. Miss Buhl had gone on down to the deck before turning back to see what was happening. Stone, last in line behind Mrs Gash, went down on one knee and pushed his hand under the instep of the wedged shoe to try to lift it free. Mrs Gash had clung onto the railing. At that moment

60

from behind the bridge had come a terrible explosion. The ship had seemed to leap out of the ocean and then tilt to one side at an ever-increasing angle. Miss Buhl, thrown to the deck, had begun to roll helplessly down the slope towards the boiling ocean.

Stone had taken the rest of the steps at a leap and had run at full tilt down the deck after her. At the last moment he had thrown himself on his belly, arms reaching to her. He had caught her wrist just as she went over the side. Her weight, together with the angle of the deck and the power of his dive, drove him forward head-first into the white upright of the railings. Through a maze of bright colours he had seen his left hand swing down the sheer black side of the ship to grasp Miss Buhl's other wrist. "I will not let go," he had thought. And then the darkness had come.

"It must be very dark, then," he said to Rebecca Dark.

"It is." There was fear in her voice. "It was OK at sunset, but a couple of hours ago the clouds started to come over, and the wind's picking up strength."

"What do the sailors say?"

"We say it's a bleedin' typhoon."

"Shut up, O'Keefe." This last, the young officer's voice – what was his name? Spooner?

"Even if it is a typhoon," continued Spooner, "there's nothing we can do about it." He spoke with calm authority. He had taken command, clearly, as was only right and proper.

Stone lay back and found that his head had been cradled in Miss Dark's lap. He sat up a little, therefore, and began to move his legs carefully and experimentally. "All right if I stand up for a moment?" he asked. "I've got cramp from lying for so long."

"Yes, certainly." Spooner's voice. "Be careful though, it's a bit choppy."

Stone put his hands on the shoulders of Miss Dark and the person seated next to her – Gant, presumably – and levered himself up off the bottom planks. The wind took him, clearing his head. It was stronger than it had seemed to be in the bottom of the boat.

Suddenly his left leg buckled, twisting with cramp. Stone toppled sideways, hopped once, waving his arms wildly, trying to regain his balance, and crashed into the side of the boat. All around him came a chorus of screams and curses. His hands slammed against the gunwale and water washed over them. Then the boat steadied and Stone eased himself inwards. "Sorry," he said.

"That's OK. No damage done." Spooner, determinedly cheerful, keeping on top of the situation. And doing it well, thought Stone as he worked himself onto a bench between two of the crew. There was still no light, but Stone could vaguely distinguish 11 shapes in the boat around him. Aft, on the after locker, sat Spooner with the gold braid on his white cap glinting every now and then. He seemed to have the tiller under his arm. God alone knew what he was steering by – perhaps he had a luminous compass. Beside him sat one of the crew – the big silent Irish American they called Slattery, to judge by his size and the width of his shoulders. Before them sat Mrs Gash and Miss Buhl. Both seemed to be asleep. On the bench in front of Stone, who was facing aft, sat Wells and two more of the crew – the little whining Irishman, O'Keefe, and the wireless operator Bates. On either side of Stone sat the huge Liverpudlian Laughton and the square Chicagoan Slobowski. Behind, on the forward locker, sat Gant and Miss Dark. "Have we checked on the provisions yet – and the radio?" Stone asked Laughton.

"Yes. This is the captain's cutter, not a proper lifeboat at all, so it wasn't equipped with a radio, but we've enough food for several days."

"No more?"

"There is enough food for 12 people for a week," said Spooner. "There is rather less water."

Stone turned back to Rebecca Dark. "What's happened?" he asked.

"After we got clear of the ship," she whispered, as though she wanted to conceal her version of events from the rest of the survivors, "Mr Spooner took charge. He said he was senior officer surviving and we must all take our orders from him. Some of the crew didn't like that but the rest overruled them and we agreed. Then we went through the things in the lockers at the front and back of the boat and sorted out all the things in them.

"There were some life-jackets, some fishhooks and line, some diesel for the engine, the food Mr Spooner mentioned, and five big five-gallon cans of water." She paused. The only sound was the lapping of the waves against the side of the boat and the heavy, rhythmic breathing of deep sleep.

Rebecca looked around the dark boat. There was no way of telling whether or not they were all really asleep, or whether they were just pretending. Still, she wasn't going to say anything they hadn't all already thought of. "There were five five-gallon cans of water, you see, but someone had made holes in them all. There's only about five gallons left that didn't leak away."

Stone sat thinking for a few minutes. "Could it have been an accident?"

"That's what we thought at first but it does seem quite clear that someone pushed a spike through the side of each one."

"It couldn't have been anything to do with the explosion?"

"No. The cupboard was dry. It must have been done days ago." She paused and then said, "I don't know, of course, but I think that if you looked in the big lifeboats you'd find the same thing."

"What makes you think that?"

"I think," said Rebecca in an almost silent undervoice. "I think someone's trying to kill us."

"Who? Why?"

"I don't know, but I am sure going to try and find out."

"But how?" asked Stone. "I mean we're in a lifeboat in the middle of the Indian Ocean. How are you going to find out here?" And then a thought seemed to occur to him. He leaned over and whispered into her ear. "You mean, whoever it was might be here with us now?"

She nodded.

Stone whistled silently and reached into his pocket for his cigarettes. The gunmetal case had saved them from the effects of his brief dip in the sea. He offered one to Rebecca and lit both. In the glow of his lighter his face showed almost vacuous concern, but in the dark he smiled grimly.

After they had finished their cigarettes they both slept. Spooner at the helm watched the brief shadowed light and the two sparks glowing and fading until they vanished into the night and the choppy sea. He was bone weary and would have given anything to be able to sleep, but he had forgotten to arrange watches – an oversight he could only excuse by reminding himself he was totally inexperienced in situations like this – and his penance was to keep watch himself. He might just as well sleep, though, for no ship would see them in this darkness and he was doing no real good just sitting here.

He had no clear idea of where they were going, which was why he had not started the engine. There was no compass. Had there been stars he could have steered by them but there were none. Tomorrow, if it cleared, they might be able to work out a rough heading by using the sun. But really, of course, that too would be a waste of time. There was nowhere for them to go.

They were perhaps 250 miles east of the African coast, but with the wind and the current steadily drifting them farther east they might as well have been 250,000 miles. To the north lay Socotra, 500 miles away, again out of reach because of the monsoon. South were the Amirantes and the Seychelles, 700–800 miles away utterly against the persistent curve of wind and current which drove relentlessly up the coast of Africa and then east across the Ocean to India.

At any other time of the year, in any other month, they might have expected the north-east trade winds to carry them onto the horn of Africa in a few days, helped by the engine. Even with five gallons of water they might have made it. But not now. Not with the south-west monsoon pushing them on to the Indian coast. If it kept up they would be swept ashore near Bombay but none of them would know anything about it. Bombay was 1,750 miles away. Even if they used the engine they would be lucky to make it in under three weeks and none of them would live more than 72 hours.

As he went to sleep there were tears in Spooner's eyes and he was angry with himself for wasting their moisture.

The storm broke just before dawn. Gant was the only person awake in the lifeboat but it took even him by surprise. What had woken him he did not know but he suddenly sprung from deep sleep into full wakefulness and sat up straight. He was stiff and sore, bones ached and muscles cramped. Rebecca's head had slipped from his shoulder into his lap and he carefully eased it onto the seat by his thigh as he turned into the pitching darkness to relieve himself over the side. When he turned back the boat was still quiet. "Mr Spooner!" he whispered, but there was no response. He debated with himself whether or not to wake the boy up for the wind seemed to be very much stronger and the waves a good deal larger. But there seemed to be nothing to be gained by making a fuss and the tall actor sat down again and was just about to try for sleep once more when the dark was shattered by the first flash of lightning, and the steady moan of the wind was lost at once in the immediate explosion of thunder.

Then the rain came and the rain was the most frightening of the three. Gant had never been in a tropical storm and had supposed that it would be like a bad thunderstorm. He was wrong. This was unimaginably worse. The rain was coming down not in drops but in wave after wave, boiling off his instantly soaking body and into the boat at an alarming rate. He tried to rise but the sheer weight of water forced him back into his seat with a crash which set the boat rocking even more wildly. He was finding it hard to breathe and had to cup one hand round his mouth and nose to stop the rain and spray drowning him.

His lower eyelids seemed to bulge and bag, painfully full of water. Even through his heavy roll-neck, his back and shoulders were bruised and he groped feverishly one-handed at his feet for his hat or anything to protect his splitting head from the terrible assault. He searched blindly because his agonized eyes were tight shut now for fear the rain would do them permanent damage. He opened his mouth to yell but even with the protection of his hand he choked on the spray and went into a racking round of coughing, gasping and choking, which stopped only when he bowed his head between his knees and covered his mouth with both hands.

Everyone else had been woken by the first clap of thunder

and most of them sat awed by the power of the storm or, like Gant, fighting a terrifying battle for breath. Only Spooner saw the most immediate danger: "BAIL! For God's sake, bail," he yelled. One or two heard him and began to do so, but too few and nearly too late. Gant tore the forward locker open and pulled out one of the spiked watercans, hoping to fill it with fresh rainwater.

Carefully amid the confusion he began to fill it from the water slopping in the bottom of the boat, keeping it always on its side with the hole, bunged by his handkerchief, uppermost. After a few moments Spooner noticed what he was doing and screamed down the boat, "Belay that and bail." Gant began to bail. The water was almost up to his knees now and he saw with sick dread that the gunwales were so near the water that wave after wave was breaking into the boat.

Stone had found an old tin cup and was bailing feverishly with that. At first he had been throwing the water anywhere so long as it went out of the boat, but he soon noticed that when he threw it into the wind it blew straight back in again. So he was half-sitting half-kneeling with his back to the storm letting the wind take the water away.

The level in the boat slowly stopped rising and the waves stopped breaking in on them. Stone at last raised his head and eased the knotted muscles of his shoulders. There was a faint light now, enough to brighten the outlines of the whirling clouds but not enough to take the dazzling edge off the jagged talons of lightning which still reached down out of the sky tearing at tired eyes with their brightness. Stone could see the unsteady figures of Spooner and Slattery as they wrestled with the kicking tiller, trying to keep the boat from drifting sideways-on to the sea and, stretching into the haze behind them, row upon row of white-fanged waves. The boat rocked back and forth like an insane see-saw as the waves roared in under her stern and out under her bow. He watched helplessly as first Miss Buhl and then even the intrepid Mrs Gash lurched forward and was rackingly seasick. He felt sick himself and looked away.

Then, infinitely wearily, he began to bail again. Bend back. Fill cup, hands shaking, water slopping over the sides of the tin. Straighten back: tearing pains from shoulders to cramped calves. Throw water: pain in his arms almost beyond bearing. Bend back. And so on. There was a rhythm to it and Stone, in spite of his weariness, began to fit the words of a half-remembered song around it:

> "I get no kick from cham-PAGNE
> Mere al-co-HOL
> Doesn't thrill me at ALL
> So tell me why should it be TRUE
> That I get a KICK
> Out of YOU?"

Slobowski looked at him strangely for a moment, and then his battered face split into a grin and together he and Stone bellowed the next lines:

> "I get no kick from a PLANE
> Fly-ing too HIGH
> With some BIRD
> In the SKY
> Is my I-
> Dea of NOTHING
> To DO
> But I I I I
> Get a KICK
> Out of YOU!"

68

By this time everybody, heartened, decided to join in:

"I get no KICK
From co-CAINE . . ."

And then the tiller snapped.

The boat lurched wildly and began to swing beam-on to the angry sea. She began to rock wildly from side to side and the waves tumbled in over the gunwales again. "An oar! Pass an oar!" yelled Spooner. The oars were stored along the length of the boat with the mast and sail under the three lateral seats. In a panic of action almost every person on board leaned down and grabbed at the smooth cylinders of wood.

"This one!" yelled Stone freeing the oar beneath himself. Eager hands found it and pulled it forward towards the bow of the boat to free it. Gant and Rebecca took it back and up until its broad blade came out from under the third bench, then they both leaned far forward as Stone, Slobowski and Laughton passed it to O'Keefe, Wells and Bates. Even Miss Buhl and Mrs Gash helped guide it back to Slattery and Spooner in the stern. Thus every person in the boat was holding some part of its 13 ft length when it suddenly gave a violent twist. The blade broke free of Spooner's grip and struck the young officer violently in the face. "Look out!" cried Wells, his voice a whisper in the wind. Slattery reached out with the reactions of a cat, but was far, far too late.

Spooner had been half crouching on the aft locker, preparing to slide the oar past the sternpost for use as an improvised tiller. The flat, iron-bound edge of the oar's blade smashed across his upper lip just below his nose. The force of it lifted him nearly erect in the pitching little boat. He took half a step backwards as tears flooded his eyes and blood was suddenly bright around his mouth and chin. His hands came up towards his face. Slattery's fingers brushed the white cotton of his trouser-leg and he fell backwards over the side.

Slattery tore the oar by main force out of their collective grasp and thrust it out to Spooner but it fell short of the struggling man. Gant wrenched a life jacket from the forward locker and hurled it into the raging water. Spooner's wildly waving arm splashed down upon it and his left hand clutched at it but his body twisted until it was facing the waves and his mouth, still wide and gasping at the pain, filled with water so that he choked.

In the boat, still frozen with horror, they watched him turn again, his face almost blue and twisted with the agony of burning throat and lungs, water spilling from mouth and nostrils as he made another almost dreamy attempt to swim towards them. But the gulf between the tossing boat and the drowning man was far too wide. Spooner stopped, distant now as the boat was swept away, and sank out of sight. For an eternal moment as they rode over the crest of a tall wave, they saw the yellow life-jacket with his hand still gripping its webbing straps. Then even that slight hold was broken and Spooner was gone.

With a vicious crash that jerked them all out of their immobility, Slattery slammed the oar down by the tree of the broken rudder. "Bail, God damn you!" he roared, and he set about lashing the oar in place.

"Dear goodness," whispered Miss Buhl, her voice lost in the roar of waves, wind and rain. Nobody else said anything. They all began to bail silently and fiercely. Slowly the boat began to turn again as Slattery's makeshift tiller took hold until eventually the great grey waves were once again combing in from her stern.

They kept it up for the next few hours as the thunder quietened and the wind moderated. At about midday the

70

wind died altogether although there was still a high sea running. They took the sudden calm as a signal to stop bailing and break out some food. As they sat, mindless with fatigue, numbly munching sodden biscuits, Gant said, "What we need is a successor for poor Mr Spooner." He spoke quietly, but his voice carried easily to every ear in the boat.

"I ain't taking no orders from no one," said O'Keefe. This time it was Slattery who told him to shut up.

"I think Mr Slattery is the obvious choice," said Wells.

"Yes," said Stone.

"I agree," said Gant. All the others nodded except for O'Keefe and Slattery himself. And so it was agreed and they all looked to Slattery for the next word. "Right," he said at last, "I see no point in rationing the food but if we're to stand any chance of surviving I'm afraid I will have to ration the water. We have five gallons."

"Nearly seven, I should say," said Gant, holding up the can he had part-filled during the storm.

"I'm afraid not, sir," said Slattery regretfully.

"But I . . ." Gant was prepared to argue.

"If you would just taste some of it, sir," suggested Slattery wearily. Stone passed Gant his tin cup and the American carefully poured out a little of the rain water. Then as they all watched him he took a sip. His face twisted and he spat hurriedly over the side. "There would have been salt in the spray, salt in the bottom of the boat, salt water everywhere, you see, sir," said Slattery apologetically.

"God!" said Gant. "I didn't realize." And they all watched him with burning eyes as he poured two gallons of clear sparkling water over the side.

"If I might have the remaining five gallons and the cup up here," asked Slattery. They were passed rapidly down the boat. "I think we'll allow you all a cupful now," decided the big Bronx Irishman, "but while the clouds are running and it's still cool we'll keep it to a minimum. When the sun comes out we'll need every drop we've got and more." One cup each used up half a gallon. "Remember," said Slattery as they finished, "we can do that nine more times. That's all."

There was silence then for a few minutes and then Wells said, "I thought I saw a water-maker in there. Shouldn't we set it up?" He gestured to the after locker.

"There'll be no use setting that up until the sun comes out," Slattery explained. "It works by sunlight you see, sir. It uses sunlight to evaporate the sea water in the first tank so that distilled water can be condensed into the second tank – the small one. But when the sun does come out I'd be glad if you will set it up. Every little helps." Wells nodded.

"There are some fish-hooks and line too," said Stone.

"Yes, sir, I was thinking of that. When the sea moderates we'll break them out. I think we've a tiny oil stove so we might have a fry-up later. In any case, if we just sit here doing nothing I think we'll all find the boredom a wearisome thing, but if we sit here doing nothing holding on to the end of a fishing line – well, that'll be *fun*." He beamed round the boat, enthusiastic, extremely Irish. "Isn't it a terrible thing what a difference a few fathoms of string and a hook will make, when you're sitting doing nothing at all?"

There were one or two rather reluctant smiles in answer to his sudden brogue, and morale began to move up again. He saw this and shrewdly continued to bolster it. "We've a ten-gallon can of diesel for the motor, but I think we'll save that in case we're too tired to row when we sight land. And we're in a strong current, it'll take the engine every drop of power we can spare just to move us across it anyway."

He paused, trying to think of something else he needed to say. "We'll need someone officially on watch all the time, and that person had better have the Very pistol.

Now, there are eleven of us so we'll take two hours each, except for Mr Slobowski and I who will take three. It's, let's see, twelve-twenty now. I'll take until three-thirty. Mr Slobowski until six-thirty, then Miss Buhl, Mrs Gash, Mr Wells, Mr Stone, then Laughton, O'Keefe and Bates, and lastly Mr Gant and Miss Dark. OK?"

They all nodded except O'Keefe.

"Right. I think that's everything. Mr O'Keefe, break out the fish-hooks. Mr Bates, some of that terrible corned beef for bait. And Mr O'Keefe, when you've done that, dry off the Primus stove if you would."

"Do this. Do that. *If I would*," muttered O'Keefe. "You'll be lucky if you don't go the way of Mr Spooner, mate." He had forgotten that everyone could hear him.

"What do you mean by that?" rapped out Gant.

"I didn't mean nothing," whined O'Keefe sulkily. Then, because everybody was looking at him, he began to defend himself. "Well, it ain't as if it was an accident, was it? I mean somebody shoved that oar, didn't they? Like, oars don't just twist on their own, you know?"

"Yes, but we must do something," said Mrs Gash, directing her dark-pouched eyes at each one in the boat in turn.

"What can we do?" asked Gant gently, leaning forward until the shadow of his hat-brim closed like a curtain down his long face.

"What do you mean, what can we do?" whined Mrs Gash petulantly.

"Well, Mrs Gash, I really see no course of action which we can follow. We are adrift in an open boat, miles from anywhere, with a murderer aboard. I myself would be hard-pressed to know what to advise even if we knew who this person was. As I do not, I find myself totally at a loss.

How, for instance, are you going to go about discovering your criminal?"

"Well, the reason for the crime is always important."

"Agreed. Has anyone any idea why Mr Spooner should have been killed?"

"Someone didn't like his face," volunteered O'Keefe.

"It's silly," said Rebecca Dark in a husky voice. "Why should anyone want to kill the man with the best chance of saving us all?"

"Simple," answered Wells. He gestured to the spiked five-gallon water can. "The person who wants us all dead."

"Oh God," said Miss Buhl, faintly.

"But that's assuming that Spooner was killed *because* he was the man with the best chance to save us," said Wells. "He might have been killed for some other reason in spite of that fact."

"This speculation is useless, you know," said Slattery. "It won't get us anywhere and it's frightening the ladies."

"Not only the ladies," said Stone, and shivered.

They had been indulging in a somewhat circular argument for over an hour now, as they chewed desultorily on the corned beef and biscuits which made up the bulk of their boat's stores. They were in the early part of Mrs Gash's watch, and as darkness began to press down on the face of the water their one concern was their safety in the night. Mrs Gash had first voiced the worry that had been nagging at the mind of everyone aboard except, presumably, that of the murderer. And now she continued. "Well, I think we should assume the worst and take precautions accordingly."

"I'm inclined to agree with that," said Slattery from among the shadows. "I think the best thing we can do just at the moment is double up on the night watches." He thought for a moment as the last paleness began to fade from the sky. "It would be simplest if you just teamed up and did four hours together. So Mr Wells and Mr Stone are on together from ten-thirty to two-thirty and then Laughton and O'Keefe until six-thirty. OK?" They all nodded, except O'Keefe who was muttering darkly about always having the graveyard watch. "Right," said Slattery. "A cup of water each now, I think, then off to sleep. I'll keep watch with Mrs Gash until ten-thirty." The water was shared out. They went to sleep.

The night was warm and in spite of the fact that there was no moon, it was very bright. The stars seemed to be bigger and more numerous than usual, hanging low and liquid in the black velvet sky. Distance ceased to have any meaning so the stars appeared to be very close indeed. The boat left a wide trail of phosphorescence in the still water which curved away to starboard, carried by the monsoon current. This line of light, now clear, now only a memory on the backs of their eyes like the Milky Way in the sky, was a particularly beautiful sight marred only by the huge dark shapes of sharks which cruised through it now and then.

At ten-thirty Slattery told Mrs Gash that her watch was finished. She prodded Silas Wells who checked his watch and prodded Stone. They worked their way aft until Wells could take the improvised tiller while Stone guarded the Very pistol. Then they sat in silence for a while. They might have sat thus all night but after a while O'Keefe stirred and worked his way forward. He relieved himself noisily and came back.

"Not asleep?" asked Stone casually.

"I'm not sleeping at night until they've caught that bloody murderer, mate, and I'd advise you to do the same. I'm just lying there wide awake. No one's going to do me in, no way."

"Well, it's your beauty sleep, O'Keefe," shrugged Wells.

"Aye and it's my life. Nobody's going to end it any

earlier than I want." Then O'Keefe lay down and to all intents and purposes went to sleep. Suddenly Wells became quite talkative: "What do you think of that? Funny sort of a fellow."

"Seems eminently sensible to me," observed Stone.

"Oh surely not. I mean the man's an absolute idiot, and quite spectacularly cross-grained into the bargain. In fact," he lowered his voice and leaned over to whisper in Stone's ear. "I'd have picked him as prime suspect."

"Why?"

"Well, I mean he wouldn't take orders from poor old Spooner. It was obvious he hated him like blazes. I bet it was a personal thing and he did it just on the spur of the moment."

"I don't think so. His sort just hate everybody. I don't think there was anything personal in it for Spooner."

"Sod off," said O'Keefe.

"The thing is," said Wells, totally disregarding the little Irishman. "If it isn't him, then who could it be?"

"Anybody."

"Yes, quite. And that puts us in rather a sticky position, doesn't it?"

"That's why there are two of us."

"Yes, but I mean there might be some way for him – or her – to creep up in the dark. I admit we both noticed O'Keefe but he was blundering about a bit. It's not so light that someone couldn't take us by surprise you know."

Stone had to admit that there was a great deal of truth in this. Indeed, half listening to Wells, he had been thinking of an acquaintance of his own who had been killed in a small boat by someone who had slid silently over the side and then popped up behind the stern armed with an extremely sharp knife. A simple scenario sprung into his mind: the killer rising silently behind them, grasping the tiller-oar for a second.

76

Two well-timed knife thrusts, turning the boat beam-on to wind and water, toppling it over so that everyone else was wet as well, then, after the confusion, where are Mr Wells and Mr Stone? Has anybody seen them? No, of course not. Vanished into the night. All so easy. He shivered.

"I was just thinking," continued Wells, "that if we lit one of the lamps I saw in the emergency stores, we could stand it between us on the seat here."

"And make ourselves a damn good target."

"Only if someone's going to shoot at us, and our murderous friend will have to be a bit more subtle than that." Suddenly they were talking the same language and each became aware that the other was not altogether what he seemed.

"Quite," said Stone dryly.

Wells got up and quietly worked his way along the length of the boat, moving with the sureness of a cat and more than amply supporting his own argument for the necessity of the lamp as protection. Stone held the rudder and kept the slight night breeze firmly on his back in case the boom should swing over and knock the journalist out of the boat.

In mid-afternoon, after the last of the heavy rainclouds had been swept out of the sky, a gentle but steady wind had sprung up. At first they had been content just to let it blow over them, cooling their baking bodies in the heat of the declining sun. But after half an hour or so, when it showed absolutely no sign of gusting out, Slattery had said, "Right. Let's get the mast stepped and put the sails up."

It had been surprisingly easy, in spite of the confusion of ropes and canvas, and by half-past four they had the two sails up and turned the little cutter into a makeshift yacht. They heeled a little to starboard as the steady little wind filled the sails and tried to push the broad deep hull through the water. A little bow wave sprang up and gurgled like a thoughtful baby beneath Gant and Rebecca.

Spirits had briefly lightened, before supper and the discussion about the murderer, with the new sense of purpose the wind had lent the little boat. There was only one danger, Slattery warned. With the wind coming in varying strengths from almost dead astern, and with the makeshift rudder only barely in control of the boat's progress, the boom was particularly easy to disturb. With the boom straining out to starboard, the slightest careless movement, the slightest re-distribution of weight which might rock the boat towards port, would bring the sail over onto the opposite tack and the heavy wooden boom would slam across the boat and could knock anyone in the way insensible or out of the boat.

Thus, now as Wells crept carefully by them in the humming dark, Mrs Gash and Miss Buhl slept on the after bench, each with her head upon some part of the other, keeping low, as Slattery had advised them to, well clear of the boom. Behind them, on the bench just aft of the mast, also keeping low to avoid the boom, also sound asleep now, lay Bates, Slattery and O'Keefe. Forward of them, before the mast, Slobowski and Laughton were more at their ease with no boom above them.

Wells wondered briefly why Slattery had gone to sleep between O'Keefe and Bates rather than coming up here. Right forward were Gant and Miss Dark, who at least looked upon Wells with a little more favour since he had saved her life.

She was still possessed only of the panties which she had put on in her stateroom just before the explosion, but had replaced Bates' heavy white jacket round her shoulders with a shirt found unaccountably floating in the water by the boat. It fitted her like a smock. Wells wondered why no one on the boat had offered her his shirt in the face of her obvious discomfort with Bates' coat. Perhaps, like Wells himself, they all had something hidden up their sleeves.

He moved her legs carefully and began to grope in the forward locker. The oil lamps were at the back. He moved Gant's legs a little also and reached right in. Suddenly Gant's hand rested on the back of his neck gently but in a grip which would incapacitate him at a moment's notice and perhaps kill him into the bargain. "What are you up to?" asked Gant quietly.

"I'm getting a lamp. Stone and I are afraid of the dark." The hand remained where it was for a moment and then was gone. "I see," said Gant, and it was clear from his tone that he did see. He spoke the same language as Stone and Wells. Was there anybody on this boat, Wells wondered, who was actually what they seemed to be? He crept back to Stone, carrying the lamp and lost in thought.

It was a tall lamp, made of bronze and glass. The reservoir was a bronze cup and a long glass nozzle protected the flame. This glass nozzle had an extremely small hole at the top, and was painted all down one side with a reflective silver paint. It was a lamp specifically designed for work such as this, the glass ensuring that the flame once lit would not easily go out, the paint capable of functing not only as a reflector multiplying the light to one side but also as an excluder cutting it off from the other side so that if necessary the lamp could be used for signalling. All in all, it was cheaper to run and more reliable even than their big flashlamp – especially considering what salt dampness could do to long-life batteries. On one side of the bowl, stencilled in black paint was the legend, "Haley's Seaman's Oil Lamp. Property of JJ Hyde and Co London. WANDERER."

Wells put it on the after locker beside Stone and lit it, using Stone's silver lighter. "Better cover your eyes from the glare," he said, narrowing his own to the merest slits. Stone closed his eyes obediently, automatically checking that the Very pistol was beside him on the bench. "OK," said Wells after a moment, "you can open up now." The brightness brought tears to Stone's eyes. He looked away.

"Gant woke up while I was getting it", continued Wells. "Are you still awake, Mr Gant?" No reply. "Must have gone over again. I must say it's rather a thrill having someone that famous aboard. I wonder, would he give me his autograph if we get out of this alive? Not such a thrill for you, I suppose. You must have worked with most of them yourself – or at least met them. I say, you wouldn't give me your autograph, would you? I don't really collect them any more, but I once had quite a good collection. Went in for it quite seriously when I was a lad.

"Theatrical, mainly, too – used to go to the theatre quite often in London you know. Good while ago now, of course, I mean I've been East for more years than I care to remember. But back to England now. If we make it, of course . . . Do you think he'd mind?"

"Mind what?"

"Giving me his autograph?"

"Don't see why he should."

"Oh, I don't know! I suppose so many people want it, he must get pretty fed up with it at times."

"Not really. You get used to it."

"Do you? I don't think I should: all those people, all wanting a piece of you. Must be pretty grim."

"Price of fame."

"I suppose so." Pause. "Well, you should know, anyhow."

"Yes."

They were silent for a while. Stone became sleepy. He was

very tired and his head still hurt a little. There was a ridge of bruising from temple to crown. Wells began gently to hum a little lullaby. Stone was finding it impossible to keep his eyes open. The warm wind whispered in the ropes, the sail flapped gently once or twice, the water gurgled distantly at the bow but whispered away from her stern. Stone's head began to droop, then it slammed up again as he forced himself awake. He lit a cigarette.

"Mind if I have one?" asked Wells.

"Sorry, didn't know you smoked."

"I don't usually, but it might help to keep me awake." Stone passed him the gunmetal case. Wells took it, removed a cigarette, and held up the case as a windbreak while he leaned forward to light the cigarette at the lamp. His movement, thoughtlessly sudden, caused the boat to give a little lurch. The tiller struck his arm. The cigarette case flew with a clatter into the middle of the boat. "Sorry," said Wells, starting up a little unsteadily, causing the boat to waver again, "I'll get it."

"It's OK," said Stone, "just hold on to the tiller here. I can get it." Wells sat down more carefully. Stone got up and went quietly down the boat. The case was beside Miss Buhl's feet and Stone crouched down to get it. As he did so, Wells gave a stifled exclamation and the boat tilted slightly. Stone looked back at him and suddenly everything went black, with a hollow thump.

Then Wells was holding him, whispering urgently. "Stone. Stone, are you all right?"

"Think so," he managed, "What happened?"

"The boom hit you."

"God! My head!"

"You'll be all right. You were only out for a second."

"Aaah!" said Stone as he moved his head.

"Sssh! You'll wake the others."

"Sorry."

"OK. Can you sit up?"

"Yes."

"Good . . . That's it. OK." They got to the locker.

"Hey! What goes on? Where's the lamp?"

"Knocked it overboard, I'm afraid. The tiller swung when I got up to help you. Knocked it overboard."

"I see."

"I don't know what did it – must have been a fluke in the wind."

"Yes. Must have."

"Still. No harm done, eh?"

"No harm done," said Stone and sat back. It had been a nasty thump. His head hurt abominably. He felt sick.

"You sure you're all right?" Wells sounded concerned.

"Yes. I suppose so."

"I tell you what. I'll wake Slattery up. There might be something in the medicine chest. If this boat has one. I mean it didn't have a radio or anything, so who knows, eh?" As he said this, he crept down the boat and shook the fatigue-drugged Slattery. "Careful you don't wake O'Keefe," he whispered to the big Irishman, "he's in a foul mood." Slattery came carefully up the boat, "What happened?"

"I bashed him on the bonce with the boom, I'm afraid: damn careless."

"No harm done, seemingly," said Slattery gently probing Stone's battered skull. "I'll break out some medicinal whisky."

He did so, and they were all three sipping it appreciatively when Slattery suddenly straightened. "What's that?" he snapped.

"Where?" said Wells.

"Out there to starboard . . . I thought . . . it looked like a light."

82

"I can't see anything." Stone.

"Seems to have gone," Slattery, puzzled.

"Optical illusion?" Wells.

"Don't think so. It looked like a light. I couldn't make it out."

"We'll keep watch," said Wells. "To starboard, you say?"

"Yes. It might have been anything, but . . . WAIT! There it is again!"

"I see it," said Stone.

There was a light away to starboard. Just for a second it glinted on the water, too bright and substantial to be a star on the horizon.

"Quick!" cried Wells, full voice now, "the Very pistol!"

"Where is it?" Stone.

"You've got it!" Wells, frantically.

"It's not on the seat." Stone.

"What's the matter?" Mrs Gash, stridently.

"There's a light." Slattery.

"Where is it?" muttered Stone to himself.

"What are you looking for?" Miss Buhl, sleepily.

"The Very pistol," snapped Stone.

By now everyone was awake. They stood by the mast and began to shout. Typically, O'Keefe, who had said he was going to stay awake, was the only one not joining in for he was sitting stolidly in his place and seemed to be still asleep.

"There it is," cried Wells, seeing a silvery column catching starlight on the little Irishman's lap. "O'Keefe's picked it up." He went over to O'Keefe and took the Very pistol from him. O'Keefe stirred. "Thanks," said Wells. Then he turned quickly and fired it into the air. The white flare curved up and away into the darkness on the port beam. Everybody was on their feet now except O'Keefe. They all shouted and yelled, moving across to one side of the boat as the light grew steadily smaller.

"Another flare, quick!" cried Laughton and there was a concerted movement towards the flare box.

"Careful!" yelled Slattery, but too late. Mrs Gash's ample form tottered and then tumbled sideways. The boat shook as she landed then tilted onto another tack. The boom swung, caught O'Keefe a solid thump on the head and pitched the little Irishman into the water. Nobody noticed.

"It's going," whispered Miss Buhl.

"Where the HELL is that flare?" shouted Slobowski.

"Here," said Wells and fired it away to starboard. Ten pairs of eyes searched the distant horizon as the flare rose and curved in the air, its long thin trail exploding suddenly into a white magnesium light. "It's gone," said Bates.

"Nothing there at all," said Gant. "What did you see?"

"Mr Slattery saw it first," said Wells, "it was a sort of a light. It was quite clear. Stone and I saw it as well."

"Yes," agreed Stone.

"Well, whatever it was, it's gone now," said Laughton. The flare sank towards the horizon.

"What's that?" suddenly cried Rebecca, whose eyes had strayed down from the falling flare.

"Sweet Jesus, it's a man," said Slattery.

"But that's impossible!" said Wells, "Where could he have come from?"

Then Bates noticed that O'Keefe was gone. "My God, it's O'Keefe," he yelled. "O'Keefe. O'KEEFE!" But O'Keefe gave no sign of having heard them. He was floating face-down some yards to starboard and he seemed to be unconscious. "Quick! Get over to him before the flare goes out," ordered Wells. Then the flare went out.

"There's a torch," said Slattery.

"Here. In this locker," said Gant. And in a few moments

it was probing the water. O'Keefe's left arm appeared first, slightly bent and quite still on the water. Then his shoulder and his head. He began to roll slightly, the waves splashing against his dark shock of hair. "He's waking up!" whispered Wells, hardly believing it, and O'Keefe began to roll over. "I'm going in," said Stone, already stripping off his jacket.

"No!" Wells. "*LOOK!*"

In the shadows behind O'Keefe, something moved. The little Irishman was galvanized into action. He jerked up, eyes wide and staring, mouth agape in a silent scream, and lurched through the water towards the boat.

"Here! Hurry!" screamed Rebecca, but O'Keefe slowed and began to drift again as though it were all too much effort for him. Behind him, at the edge of the circle of light, more dark shapes moved restlessly. The water became agitated and O'Keefe began to roll into some sort of swimming stroke but the sharks whirled around him, their evil slit mouths moving closer and closer.

"No! Oh God, NO!" cried Rebecca.

"Do something!" screamed Mrs Gash. The first of the long shapes flashed by O'Keefe's tossing head. The man in the water reared his chest clear of the surface. The tiger sharks closed in.

Suddenly the beam of the torch dipped, then rose and steadied. There came six pistol shots fired so quickly that they were almost one long explosion. Everyone turned, momentarily forgetting O'Keefe. In the bows of the boat, steadied on widespread legs, Eldridge Gant stood with a blue snub-nosed Smith and Wesson .38 Police Positive revolver. He held it directly over the torch aiming both as if he had been well trained.

They all stood silent and immobile as the smoke curled into the torch beam, coloured blue-white like cigarette

85

smoke, and the echoes died flatly on the water. Then there came a strange dead sound part way between a splash and a thump. O'Keefe jerked erect, his hands thrown up into the air. A red-brown stain blossomed behind him. Miss Buhl fainted just as the second shark struck. It took O'Keefe below the waist and his body was wrenched under the surface. After a second, however, the torso bobbed up again, falling forward with the weight of the head. Then, strangely, it jerked fully upright again and started to move rapidly through the water. The head bounced grotesquely, nodding and rolling. The hands slapped on each wave as though applauding the performance.

But then it ended. The last shark took what was left of O'Keefe from below. Suddenly the water erupted beneath the wildly careering torso and it was taken up and up and up into the air, cradled in the gaping maw of a great grey-brown tiger shark. For a second it seemed to hang there like some fabled monster with the head and torso of a man, and the tail of a shark. But then there was a sharp crackling like dry wood being snapped as O'Keefe's ribs were crushed, the tawny body smashed back into the ocean and was gone.

Eldridge Gant switched off the torch and put his gun away.

Stone sat and watched them in the bright dawn light. It was going to be a hot day, he thought, not looking forward to it: hot and bright and clear. They were all awake – indeed he doubted whether anyone had slept at all after Gant had plunged them back into welcome darkness. They were all awake but they sat stunned by fatigue and fear, silent and haggard. Even the huge figures of Slattery and Laughton seemed to have shrunk and the Englishman's placid face was pale. Stone reached up to scratch his beard, prickly and itching with two days' growth, and all their eyes swivelled suspiciously towards the movement.

Stone wondered if this was in fact the murderer's objective: certainly if they wanted to continue their campaign it was hard to think of better circumstances to do so than those of mutual fear and mistrust. Stone stirred uneasily. The words Wells had flippantly uttered in answer to Miss Dark's question earlier took more force in his mind as he thought: Perhaps someone did want them all dead. Why? Insufficient information.

On the face of it, yes: insufficient. But what information did he actually have? Take Gant, for instance: World-famous actor, widely travelled, unmarried, unattached. Capable of quick action. Even, according to that article in the *Straits Times* a couple of days before they sailed, a Vietnam veteran, ex-Special Forces. Armed with a heavy little gun he knew how to use. Motive? Insufficient evidence. Miss Dark, Wells, Slobowski, Laughton, Bates, Miss Buhl, Mrs Gash and Slattery. Insufficient evidence. Insufficient information. Nothing.

Stone stirred discontentedly. He hated inaction but there was nothing to be done. He coughed. They all stared at him suspiciously.

The sun came up over the horizon, gold rays striking like arrows across the quiet sea. They all stirred and shifted, slitting eyes and licking lips. Stone had a sudden illusion in the yellow dawn that he was surrounded by Chinamen.

"I think," said Slattery, his voice made harsh by the dryness of his throat, "it's time for breakfast." All the yellow slit-eyed faces turned towards him. Nobody spoke. "Today's menu consists of corned beef, corned beef or corned beef." Nobody thought it was funny. Bates wearily began to open cans. Slattery brought the five-gallon can of water out of the after locker. "One cup each, remember." He poured out a cup and handed it to Miss Buhl, who took it and began to drink avidly. She had taken a couple of swallows when she dropped the cup and began to retch.

"What's the matter?" Mrs Gash leaned over her solicitously.

"Salt," gasped Miss Buhl.

"Oh CHRIST!" said Wells in an undervoice. Stone's mouth went dry. Slattery held up the can and took a careful sip. His face screwed up. He spat. "Salt," he said, and the word echoed around the boat like a funeral bell: Salt. Salt. Salt. It might just as well have been arsenic, thought Stone. And the sun was suddenly very hot indeed. "What about the water-maker?" asked Gant, an undertone of strain even in his calm New England voice. The water-maker was in the after locker and it was untouched. "Thank God," said Mrs Gash.

"I don't think God had a lot to do with it," said Gant. Stone looked at the water-maker in considerable surprise. He had really not expected it to be there. Now here was a rather complex puzzle. The murderer wanted them to die but did not want them to die. Or wanted some to die and not others. But if the murderer wanted some to survive then this was a rather imprecise method of going about it. Wasn't it?

Stone sat trying to make sense out of it while Wells filled the water-maker in the sea. Nobody ate any of the dry meat and biscuits. "I say," said Wells, "Shouldn't we check among the tins in there and see whether there are any tins of fruit? I mean, they might have something with a bit liquid in them." Right at the bottom of the Provisions box, which nobody had thought of emptying until that moment, were three large tins of Australian cling peaches, 'The Sunshine Fruit', and three large tins of mandarin oranges. Bates opened a tin of each and they had breakfast after all.

The air of relief and new confidence which grew out of this piece of good fortune withered quickly in the heat of the sun. There was a slight, steady wind but although it served to tilt the boat and fill the sail it could not take the heat out of the merciless day. They covered themselves against the sun as best they could, taking special care to protect their heads and necks. But Miss Buhl had on a sleeveless dress and she had to sit in the shade of the sail until midday when there was no shade left. Rebecca Dark was also in trouble for the shirt which covered her body did nothing to protect her legs. Stone gave her his jacket which he had been wearing like a turban, and sat in the shade of the sail with Miss Buhl.

By midday they were all prostrate. Breathing was a chore and any other movement virtually impossible. The only sounds were the fitful whisper of the wind in the rigging, the inane bubbling of the water under the bows and the deliberate, maddening, drip-drip-drip of the water-maker. Stone forced his mouth closed and made himself breathe steadily through his nose in a vain attempt to conserve body moisture. Reality began to recede and a whirlpool of exhaustion gripped him. The pyramid point of the sail wavered across the white hot disc of the sun.

The pale blue sky seemed terribly far away.

He tossed restlessly and the terrifying size of the ocean almost overwhelmed him. Stone found his back suddenly wedged hard against the tilted mast, the sail billowing over his shoulder. The infinite surface of the sea mocked him, light concealing depths, and, to his mind which was wildly spiralling out of control now, monsters of incredible size and savagery. Great white sharks, longer than the boat, which would crack the craft like a nutshell. Huge killer whales could crush it like a pea. Wild visions of huge squids, manta rays, all the childhood panoply of ocean terrors, reared before him. The oily round of each wave magically transformed into the back of some kraken let loose to destroy the world.

"What are you doing?" Slattery. It was little more than a whisper but it was as good as a shout. Stone opened his eyes. Wells was sitting with a flask at his lips, frozen in the act of drinking. "What is that?" Slattery demanded, concern giving some strength to his voice. Wells looked around the boat, his gaze switching guiltily from one hostile pair of eyes to another. He gulped, suddenly pale. "I'm sorry," he whispered, "I didn't realize."

"*What is it*?" Slatery pulled himself to his feet and went over to Wells so unsteadily as to make the boat rock.

"It's only my whisky," said Wells and offered it to him. "Have a taste."

"No thank you, sir. I'm not a drinking man," said Slattery ponderously.

"But I thought you were Irish," exclaimed Wells in frank astonishment.

"We don't all behave according to our national characteristics, sir. May I just let Mr Stone have a taste to check?" But he was already giving it to Stone as he spoke. "Don't take too much of that, sir, it will make you thirsty."

"A sniff will be enough. Yes. That's whisky allright."

"Sorry to have caused so much of a commotion, sir," said Slattery.

"No, no. That's allright. My fault entirely. I'm afraid I didn't think."

"Well. No harm done. But if I were you, I wouldn't drink too much of that: send you off your head."

"No. Just a sip or two – medicinal purposes, eh?" But

for all the good it seemed to do him he might just as well not have bothered.

Later, Bates gestured to the water-maker. "I think there's enough for a mouthful all round," he whispered.

"Right," grated Slattery's dust-dry voice, "Pour it into the cup and pass it round."

"Ladies first," said Bates and handed it to Mrs Gash. She took a sip and nudged Miss Buhl. Miss Buhl toppled off her seat and slumped in a heap on the boards at the bottom of the boat.

"Letty! Letty, what is it?" cried Mrs Gash. Miss Buhl moaned faintly. "Give me the water," ordered Stone, taking her head in the crook of his arm. "It must have been the salt she drank. I'm going to give her enough of this water to bring her round, OK? If I don't she'll be dead within a couple of hours."

"None of that!" suddenly growled Slobowski, his dark Polish eyes red-rimmed and glittering like buttons. "If you give it all to her, the rest of us'll be dead." He heaved himself erect. Slattery yelled, "Slobowski!" but it was far too late. The big Pole took a shambling half-step across the boat, hands reaching out for the cup. Stone, entangled with Miss Buhl couldn't move. Gant hauled himself erect by grasping the foresail, only to be knocked back by Slobowski's shoulder. The boat tilted dangerously. Slobowski grabbed the cup. Bates, giving a roar of rage and jealousy, leapt for the big Chicagoan.

Within five seconds of Slobowski's first mad outburst, the cup was spinning away into the sea, spilling out the precious quicksilver water in a rainbow spray of drops into the air. And the water-maker, ground carelessly underfoot had become a mess of crystal shards in the bottom of the boat.

Stone looked down at it more in sorrow than in anger. It

made no difference now. They were all dead. The murderer had succeeded almost in spite of himself. But he had committed suicide now too. If he – or she – had salted the water but spared the water-maker to give themselves a chance of survival once the rest of them were dead, then that chance also was gone now. Silence held the boat. Even the wind had dropped. This is it, thought Stone. A tremendous frustration welled up in him. He shook with black rage. But there was nothing to be done. This was the end.

He looked up from Miss Buhl's dead-white, salt-caked face, dragging his gaze away from the great fatigue-bruises of her eyes, and let his own eyes stray away over the glittering water to the horizon.

And fatigue, hunger, thirst all vanished under a wave of disbelief. Yet he never for a moment doubted what he saw. There was no doubting his eyes, no closing them, no rubbing them. There was no mistaking that long wedge-shaped half-shadow although he had never seen it before. Generations of seafaring ancestors stood behind him guiding his gaze and informing his mind. So Stone yelled at the top of his broken voice: "Land! *I see land*!"

Chapter Six

The Lessons

Beijing, 19–20 July

After Feng's death the Bee had nothing further to do. Restless because he was alone, increasingly feeling the loss of his partner the Hummingbird, and the dearth of decadent Western amusements he had become used to, he prowled the sand-swept city keeping in sporadic touch with headquarters in Bowstring Alley. Socially and physically he was an outsider, even though idealogically this was his home. The hours stretched out unbearably towards one full day.

He was asleep in the makeshift office he had set up on the third storey of the tall building in Bowstring Alley when the message from *Glorious Revolution* came through. The *Wanderer*, the subject ship, had vanished. There had been no mayday, no call for aid, no messages at all. She had simply vanished from the radar screen a little time before a typhoon had hit. At first bad weather had been blamed but when things cleared there was still no sign of her. There was one other ship in the area, an American vessel, the *Lincoln*, but she had seen no sign of the *Wanderer*.

The Bee read the message. He re-read it, stunned. Something had gone terribly wrong. There should have been a mayday, a derelict ship, a complete complement of passengers and crew. There should have been the

Hummingbird safe and sound. There should have been no American vessel. There should have been no silence, no empty ocean. The Bee felt fear for the first time in many years. Stark terror in fact: not for himself of course, but for his action and, almost totally, for the Hummingbird.

The Chinese Secret Service, the SAD, being younger in this last re-incarnation, but far older in fact than any other, is not as highly structured as the CIA, the FSS, or the British Secret Service. It does, however, have a rigid hierarchy of power and responsibility. The Bee had set this action up. He was the ultimate control. It was not his place to become directly involved.

Within half an hour of receipt of the message, however, the Bee was on his way to the *Glorious Revolution* in the middle of the Indian Ocean.

Moscow, 20 July; Tanzania 21 July

From his window Deputy Director Andropov could see clearly across Dzerzhinsky Square. If he craned a little to his right he could almost see the Bolshoi Theatre in nearby Sverdlov Square, but the National Hotel and the Intourist Hotel were also hidden from view. Had the building behind the GUM department store been a little smaller, he thought, or his office a few stories higher, he might be able to see Red Square in the summer when it was not snowing, raining or foggy, and feast his eyes upon St Basil's Cathedral.

Dzerzhinsky Square was full of people. It was, after all, midsummer and the height of the tourist season. Yuri Andropov clasped his hands behind his back and studied the ant-like creatures scurrying below. It was easy enough to tell who the tourists were – when they thought their guides weren't looking they directed half-fearful glances

94

up at this building. Muscovites never bothered, even now – they knew all they would ever need to know about the Lubianka, once a feared prison, now a home for many of the Federal Security Service employees.

Andropov was a big, square, brown man. A bear, his wife called him and a bear he seemed to be. But his heavy physique, his lined and lived-in face, his open, honest, twinkling eyes hid a razor mind. He had been Deputy Director of the FSS since the days of Gorbachev when it was still the KGB, a force to be reckoned with. And yet he was waiting, after his normal working hours, for a junior officer. Not just any junior officer: one of Department V's vicious little thugs. In the bad old days Department V had been known as Department 13 of the Second Chief's Directorate. Before that NKVD. What James Bond once called SMERSH in the days when the FSS had a department reading Bond books and experimenting with the secret weapons they described. Department V: the biggest army of thugs and assassins in the world.

There was a knock at the door.

"Come!" called Andropov. There was the sound of a door opening and closing. That was all. A tram threaded its way through the square, sparking like pale lightning, rumbling like an earthquake, past the empty plinth where the statue of Feliks Dzerzhinsky had stood five years ago. When Andropov turned round the man was standing to attention in front of his desk. The man looked, if anything, American. He had crew-cut light brown hair, a bland, open face, ingenuous blue eyes. He was wearing European casual clothes.

"Name? Rank?" snapped Andropov.

"Beria. Major. Department V, sir." The change of title from KGB to FSS had not occasioned much internal restructuring – or much movement of personal, for that matter.

95

Andropov pondered it for a while and then said, "Sit down please, Major." Beria sat, still at attention. Andropov rested his bear's body in the chair behind the desk and began to brief Beria on the situation as he saw it. "Some weeks ago, the Chinese border suddenly slammed shut. How many extra divisions they moved up no one could assess, but the activity there was considerable. We replied in kind, expecting some sort of incident. We even pulled some Spetsnaz out of Chechnya but there was nothing. Within a fortnight most of their men had vanished again, leaving extra guards at the more obvious crossing points. The inference is obvious: somebody was running and they thought he was running to us. Now we were not expecting any defections – even taking into account the number of people we trained, before your time, who were streamlined out of their jobs in January.

"Under these conditions our obvious ploy was to alert our Far East networks to watch out for a runner – for clearly if he was not running to us, then he was running south. We did not get anything definite but there was a considerable stirring of activity in Hong Kong. Even more than we would have expected because of the handover. One of the CIA's fleet of ocean-going ships appeared, waited for 36 hours, then sailed for Singapore. Several of the CIA Hong Kong Local Station appeared unexpectedly, then dropped out of sight. They do not seem to have gone back to Langley. They simply vanished. So what we obviously have is someone coming out of China and running through the New Territories during the last days before the handover.

"It loses focus after that, I'm afraid, except that something of great importance must still be going on. Come." He rose and walked to the wall opposite the window. On this there was pinned a large map of the Indian Ocean. "Look," he said. He pointed to two brightly coloured pins. "This," a yellow pin in the most northerly position, "is the *Glorious Revolution*, a Chinese freighter. This," a blue pin away to the south-east, "is the CIA's ship, the *Lincoln*."

"Yes sir?" Beria was not quite with him.

"Watch." Andropov brought out two plastic discs. He put them with their centres on the two bright pins. The discs overlapped slightly. "These discs represent the extreme ranges of the radar equipment we could expect these ships to be carrying."

"I see, sir . . ." Beria almost understood.

"At the point they overlap, here," Andropov pointed with a great square finger, "there has been for a fortnight and more, a ship. The British merchant vessel *Wanderer* owned by J.J. Hyde of the South Indian Line. A powerful man, with powerful friends – but that is beside the point. Three days ago, to our best computation, that ship vanished."

"Vanished, sir?"

"Pouf! Gone. Sunk. Vanished."

"But what has this to do with us, sir?"

"This is obviously a major intelligence action involving the SAD and the CIA. The Chinese obviously expected us to be involved also. And something has clearly gone wrong anyway. So it is the will of our masters that we take a closer look. Perhaps the Chinese were correct: perhaps we should be involved. At the very worst we should be able to steal a crumb or two from the table . . ."

Beria said, "I see, sir." And at last he did.

Just south of Dar es Salaam the coast of Tanzania bulges out and then swings in again just before the small town of Kisiju, some 40 miles from the capital. At 2230 local time on the evening of 21 July, two men stood on a low foreland at the outermost edge of this bulge looking out to sea. One was of medium height, a man of contained violence and quiet. The other was a great rumpled bear of a man, bigger but not so hard looking. The shorter man stood without moving, his cold blue eyes searching the moon-silvered water. The two men were obviously tourists and their colourful shirts and well-cut, expensive slacks proclaimed them to be Americans. The taller one looked at his American watch. "Half past ten, they said?" he asked in a gentle, mid-west accent.

"Half ten," said the other like a New Yorker. Both spoke English.

Andropov nodded and went back to watching the sea. Yuri Beria was not a talkative man, he had discovered. There was nothing hostile about his silences, they were often friendly: but they were still silences and Andropov preferred to talk. This was natural of course for Beria was a field agent, given and trained to silence. Andropov was an intelligence officer trained to communicate and question. Each recognized the difference and respected it. "Hot," said Andropov. Beria nodded, sweat glistening on his forehead.

They had travelled here surprisingly quickly, thanks to British Airways. Immediately after Andropov had explained the position to Beria they had left the office, arriving at Moscow's Sheremetevo Airport at 1640. At 1725 they were off to London on a BA Boeing. They arrived at London Heathrow at 1915, local time, just in time to change onto another BA Boeing which left for Dar es Salaam at 1945. Beria had slept, catlike. Andropov had chatted easily to the other passengers and the stewardesses. They arrived in Dar at 2140, local time.

They had spent the next day looking at the city. At 2100 they had driven south. It had taken them just over an hour to make the rendezvous point and they had been looking out to sea ever since.

98

"There!" said Beria suddenly, in Russian, "*Tam!*"

A small dark boat on the silver sea, silently coming in. They went down to the water's edge. Beria took out a torch and flashed it around as though he were looking for something. It had been decided not to use a code or signal on the torch as this might easily be seen. The boat came onto the shore. Fat, black inflated rubber bows whispering onto sand. "We are looking for Dar," said a voice in English.

Beria said in English, "I believe it is ten miles to the south."

The man in the boat answered. "I heard it was ten miles inland."

Andropov: "No. It is on top of a hill." Then they got into the boat and it put out to sea. Nobody said anything until the man in the bows said in Russian, "Stow your oars."

It had been decided that engines would be too noisy and might attract attention. They stowed their oars and slowly slid up beside a high steel conning-tower. There was a ladder. Beria climbed it. Andropov followed. The boat was pulled out of the water and deflated. The two agents climbed down into brightness inside the submarine.

"Welcome Major, Deputy Director," said the submarine's captain. "I am Commander Markov." They walked back down the submarine to let the crew of the boat come in. "I have received my orders. There is nothing for you to do. Yet."

Behind them the second officer said, "Dive," and the deck began to cant beneath their feet as Markov led them aft.

Washington D.C., Indian Ocean, 21 July

When the light above the open door changed from red to green and the British Flight Lieutenant struck him on the shoulder screaming, "GO!" over the devil's roar of the slipstream, Lydecker closed his eyes and took a good leap forward into space. The thunder of the RAF Nimrod fell away above him in the windy dark. He thought, I must count to three and then pull the ripcord: *three*!

"One!"

Twelve hours earlier Abe Parmilee had slammed his great square, freckled hand against the top of his desk. It was a gesture of frustration tinged with guilt. There had been no sign of *Wanderer* for nearly four days. Parmilee had known that something was wrong, and hadn't covered it sufficiently. If people were dead then he bore some responsibility because he hadn't done enough. He was not going to make the same mistake again. "On your way, Ed," he said.

0405 Eastern Standard time, Lydecker had slammed the door of his classic red Stingray, reversed it out of his parking place in the Langley complex and roared out towards the George Washington Memorial Parkway. At 0417 he came off the Capital Beltway burning rubber and watched the lights of Dulles Airport streaming towards him like a tidal wave. A minute later he heard the roar of immensely powerful engines illegally polluting the soundwaves above his head. At 0426 he got out of the Stingray, jammed his identification under the nose of the parking attendant and raced onto the main concourse.

"Paging Mr Lydecker. Mr Lydecker. Would Mr Lydecker please come to the *static*, would Mr Lydecker please come to the main Information Desk . . ."

At the information desk was a young airforce pilot. "This is supposed to be secret," said Lydecker.

"Sorry, sir: Couldn't think of a quicker way to get you."

Lydecker looked in faint disbelief at the tall, angular twin-tailed shape of the USAF F15C Eagle two-seater standing on the apron like something out of *Top Gun*. "Limit to how secret you can be in one of these anyway," said the pilot. In five minutes, Lydecker was crammed uneasily and very uncomfortably into the back seat: 0445 the Eagle leaped into the air and broke the law once more over the Arlington National Cemetery, the Pentagon and the Jet Foundation.

"Two!"

Over Dover, Delaware, they broke the sound barrier. Lydecker was still trying to pull his mind up off the runway, and the runway was a long way behind. By 0515 Eastern Standard Time, the East was long gone. By 0525 they were at 40,000 ft and it was dawn up here. Lydecker tried to sleep, but the noise kept wakening him, F15s are not made to be slept in. Nevertheless, he missed the Atlantic in a fitful doze.

Over Casablanca it was 1145, though Lydecker's watch still only said 0645, when, incredibly, a huge shadow passed over the Eagle. Lydecker jerked awake. All he could see at first was the sky, steel blue darkening to cobalt at the lower edge of space. Then, with terrifying suddenness, there was a great silver jet so close that he felt he could reach out and touch it. Behind the jet, looming in front of them, was a long tube with a cone on the end trailing out into the air like a strange kite. The Eagle nuzzled up to this, a baby at the breast, supped its fill and fell away. For a moment Lydecker saw the Sahara like a child's sandpit far below. "Next stop the Omani Airforce Base at Masirah. We'll start down in an hour," said the pilot.

101

"Three!"

At 5,000 ft the F15 had gone over on its side on the final approach to Masirah, and Lydecker watched the unsteady Persian Gulf with the angle of Muscat and Oman wobbling in the distance, then they levelled off and swooped down. The landing gear went out. The nose came up. The ground thumped Lydecker in his numb backside.

The parachute brake slammed taut behind them and the world slowed to a stop, at long last.

Lydecker looked at his watch. Coming up for 0800, only here of course it was eight hours later than that. He wound it on until it said 0455. The cockpit opened. Heat came down on him like a blanket soaked in boiling water. A young man leaned in. He had a freckled face, flaking with sunburn.

After all the frantic speed there was a hitch – the tail-end of a typhoon in the area. Lydecker got three hours' unexpected but very welcome, sleep, then they led him to the RAF Nimrod on a training mission with the Omani airforce. He climbed aboard, waving to the F15's pilot whose voice drifted lazily across the runway, saying, "It'll never fly."

In the big old aircraft he fell asleep once more in spite of the Rolls Royce engines pulling the modified Comet into the air. He just curled up on one of the basic, skeletal seats and let the fatigue claim him.

And then suddenly the Flight Lieutenant was shaking him. Together they forced his stiff body into a black wetsuit and fitted a parachute to his back as the jet swept low and the cabin de-pressurized. They smeared shark-repellent onto the black rubber. The Flight Lieutenant opened the door and yelled above the hurricane slipstream, "When the light changes you jump. Count three and pull the cord. Got that? THREE!" Lydecker nodded. The light

102

changed. Lydecker jumped and started counting: "*ONE!
TWO! THREE!*"

"Now!" He pulled the ripcord. The night jerked upright.
He looked down. The *Lincoln* lay quite stark in the white
light of the RAF's flares. Hannegan's helicopter like a toy
on her foredeck. The wind was pushing him towards her.
A small boat slid away from her side unsteadily in a fairly
high sea. When he hit the water, Lydecker slapped the chest
release of the parachute harness ("HMG would like it back
if possible, sir," the Flight Lieutenant had said) and swam
free. It sank like a stone. Then the boat was beside him.

"You Lydecker?" asked one of the junior officers who
had not met him in Hong Kong.

"You want to see my card, mister?" snarled Lydecker.
He was on board in 20 minutes, drinking rye and stinking
of shark repellent in the Captain's cabin with Hannegan as
the *Lincoln* butted north towards Socotra.

London, 22 July

The two young men almost danced around each other,
striking and parrying, stabbing and dodging. The tall,
dark one had the reach but the shorter blond had better
technique. They were evenly matched. Their loose white
shirts were marked with sweat, their hair flat, their faces
glistening with it. The swords rang like bells and the daggers
hissed. They grunted and mouthed and danced and dodged
but Nash was watching the King.

The King looked carefully around his court: they were
all watching the bout. The King leaned forward and his
left hand stole over the goblets before him. White powder
drifted down into one like snow.

"One!"

"No!"

"Judgement!"

There was blood on the dark man's sleeve. A courtier minced forward and looked: "A hit, a very palpable hit." The King's hand was back in his lap snatched away at the first hoarse call. The wounded duellist shrugged the courtier off. "Well – again."

The King rose.

Nash came forward in his seat, as he always did, sweat upon his own brow, anticipating . . .

"Stay," said the King. "Give me a drink. This pearl is thine. Here's to thy health." To the panting blond duellist. Then an impatient gesture with the left hand to the goblet poisoned with the powder: "Give him the cup." But the blond man shook his head and spoke in beautiful resonant measured tones. Nash hardly listened, slumped back in his seat, lost in frustration with the King until the swords began to ring once more. And then a pause. More dialogue. Nash opened his eyes. The Queen was on her feet now, dark, feminine, gentle and beautiful.

"The Queen carouses to thy fortune," said the Queen. The King, whose eyes had been elsewhere, looked fondly round upon her. Then his face went white. His eyes widened. His lips parted, trembling. His left hand stole to the great jewel at his throat. He half rose and stood silent, watching the bright goblet in her hand and riven with horror. "Good madam," said his nephew-son, enjoining her to drink.

The King's voice was rain on dead leaves, it was wind in old bones, it held infinities of agony in its whisper: "Gertrude, do not drink."

But she laughed. Her laugh was everything of life that the King's voice was of death. She raised the goblet to her eyes and mocked her husband lovingly. "I will, my lord; I pray you pardon me." Nash held onto the arms of the

104

seat as he always did now. He closed his eyes because he did not want to see the King's face but he saw it in his mind more clearly, wrenched away from his wife's warm gaze and touched already with death and with damnation saying, "It is the poisoned cup. It is too late."

A hand took Nash gently by the shoulder. Nash got up. They went slowly down the darkened aisle. The swords were ringing and hissing with a more deadly purpose now. A pause, and then again. Nash looked at Greenglass, "Part them, they are incens'd!" cried someone distantly.

They reached the tall dark wood doors. Nash reached out and stopped, frozen by a scream: "Look to the Queen there, ho!" Then he swung the door open, Greenglass huge behind him. He half closed his eyes against the brightness of the foyer lights. The doors were swinging closed behind them. One last despairing cry: "Oh my dear Hamlet – the drink, the drink!"

Thump-thump the doors closed. Nash took a deep breath. Another. "Come on," said Greenglass. And they went out into the night.

In Greenglass's big green Frontera, Nash asked, "What is it?"

"You'll see." Greenglass switched on the radio.

Sinatra sang: "And I will take the wine . . ." Strings rising, fading. Silence. "Heart FM," came the station ID jingle, "From the Heart of London . . ."

At No 21 Queen Anne's Gate, Greenglass stopped the vehicle and let Nash climb out. Even though he had gone to the Barbican alone and was seated in the stalls rather than the dress circle, Nash's long lean body was clothed in black evening wear, perfectly pressed and immaculate from black bow-tie to patent shoes. He drew himself fully erect, his rigid back and clipped moustache giving him a decidedly military air. He entered No 21, showing his ID and nodding easily to the uniformed doorman in the booth, then he went through a complex of passages, up in a lift at least once, rising into the Broadway Buildings at the back of which No 21, Queen Anne's Gate is situated.

In 1914 Sir Mansfield Cumming was chief of M16. He signed himself with his initial 'C'. Since then each of his successors as head of the Secret Intelligence Service has also been known as 'C'. C was waiting in Nash's office. He looked worried. He would have to be to send for Nash in the middle of the RSC's new production of *Hamlet*. It had to be that thing in the Indian Ocean. Hyde making waves about his boat. Nash waited in silence for the man to begin.

"Look," said C, "it's this business in the Indian Ocean." He lapsed into silence. Years of experience had taught him that unless your ideas were precisely and perfectly formulated, they should not be uttered. "As you know, I got a standard Action Report from the Cousins when they set up this defection in Hong Kong." He stopped again. Nash stood easily, almost at attention. He was fifty-five, fit and hard. He had spent years as a field agent, earning his place in the desk-bound hierarchy with more merit than most. "Then of course we received due notification when the centre of action moved to Singapore, and that ship of Jimmy Hyde's became involved. What's it's name?"

"*Wanderer*, sir."

"Yes. That's it: *Wanderer*. Well, you will remember we had a very full discussion about that: whether there was any real clandestine involvement there . . ."

"Yes, sir."

"Quite. We ruled it out of course. We didn't have enough to go on, and quite frankly the idea of an old freighter packed full of agents . . . well, it's all very *Maltese Falcon*, somehow. Very James Bond. So. It was a sound decision.

106

Sound. But incorrect I fear. You know the ship vanished five days ago?"

Nash nodded once: of course he knew.

"Yes," said C. "Well, what was at first sight a relatively innocent situation is becoming rapidly compromised. Quite apart from the presence of the *Lincoln* 'by coincidence' in the same theatre, not to mention that Chinese freighter, we have a known American agent going through Masirah on the Indian Ocean coast of Oman. Lydecker – local case officer on the Hong Kong fiasco. And there have been two known Federal Security Service men going through Heathrow heading for Dar es Salaam, and all points East I have no doubt. A thug from Department V called Beria and Andropov the Bear himself.

"It's beginning to look as though something important is going on, with which we want to become involved at a high level. So, I'd just like you to slip out there, my boy, and see what's to be done. I don't mind telling you it should keep Jimmy Hyde quiet, and stop his bleating about insurance and whatnot, but much more importantly it'll give you a chance to nursemaid your man on the spot. Quick thinking, that, getting him thrown out of Singapore so he would end up on the boat. What was his name again? Your executive's name?"

"Stone," said Nash. "His name is Alec Stone."

107

Chapter Seven

The Island

19–24 July

At first when Stone yelled that he could see land nobody moved. Then, incredibly, came the wild cry of a seagull and a beating of black wings above them. It was so sudden and so loud it cut through even Miss Buhl's unconsciousness and she cried out, jerking them all out of their immobility.

"Quick," ordered Slattery, "Bates, start the engine."

Bates yelled, "The diesel! Where's the fuel can?"

"Here!" Wells said.

"The rest of you." Slattery, his voice breaking. "Get the mast and sails down and stowed. Lively! For God's sake!" The wind and current were already pulling them away from the shadow on the horizon.

"Oh HURRY, Mr Bates!" gasped Miss Buhl.

Bates' hands were shaking so much he began to spill the fuel.

"Here," said Stone, and the big Englishman knelt beside the radio operator and, with the same distanced, self-aware gestures with which he had stopped his own hands shaking in the bar on the *Wanderer*, he steadied the can and together they poured the dark thick diesel fuel into the engine.

Within a couple of minutes the engine coughed into life, and Stone relinquished the fuel can to lend a hand at stowing the mast. As the propellor bit and the boat's motion attained a new, steadier purpose, Slattery swung the fat bow round and everyone looked forward. Only the silver sea like silk under the hot copper bowl of the sky.

"It's gone," said Gant wearily.

"We'll pick it up again," promised Slattery between his teeth. Rebecca half closed her eyes against the vicious glare and scanned the horizon from the bow, moving from port to starboard quarter and back again. "Something . . ." she said. She pointed away towards the starboard. There was a sort of a cloud, distant and indistinct. Her hand came back to push a strand of hair behind her ear.

"What is it?" Her tense voice matched her nervous gesture. Stone's long hand rested lightly on her shoulder. He shaded his stinging eyes, and waited for his vision to clear. The cloud resolved itself into hundreds of individual specks. A fluke in the wind brought a sound like thousands of children screaming.

"Seabirds. Make for them," he said. Slattery swung the tiller farther over, the bows came round a little more and they began to battle their way across the monsoon current towards the black column of birds. The waves, following the wind, now on their starboard quarter, made the boat pitch and yaw and drove it even more strongly towards India.

The spray, whipping up over the gunwales and soaking all of them as they gazed anxiously forward, would have been entirely welcome in the baking afternoon were it not so salty. Each of them had to make a conscious effort of massive proportions not to lick their parched and swollen lips when the icy drops rained down on them.

It took nearly 20 minutes to get back in sight of the land, and even when they could see it, Slattery had to steer nearly 20 degrees away from it into the wind and current in order to stand any chance at all of making a landfall. It was slow work at a time when the waiting was at its worst. The afternoon poured all its vicious heat upon them. Thirst, with no immediate hope of relief, burned ever more powerfully. A damp cloth over the head – re-soaked once every five minutes and bone dry again within that time – became as much of a Tantalus' Hell as the cool spray on their lips. But at least now they could see their goal.

The black shadow became a wedge shape, clear-edged, absolute. And yet the outline cloaked the reality. What would they find when they arrived? None of them doubted that it was an island. It could not be a promontory of any kind, for they all knew well enough that there were no major land masses here. But what would the island be like? There was no discussion, no excited chatter of speculation. Each of them in their own mind imagined an infinite variety of islands and oscillated between wild hope and steely despair. Would it be inhabited? Probably not. Would there be – most urgently – fresh water? Perhaps. At worst it would be a barren rock deep in stinking guano with only foetid pools of sea-spray further poisoned by bird-droppings. At best there might be a stream, some trees, some shade and hope of survival.

Either way, thought one of them, the deaths would continue, methodically and in secrecy.

Six hours later, as the sun set behind them, they were turning north-east again to let the wind and current carry them up on their final approach. They came in from the south-west, therefore, catching a glimpse of great dark cliffs away to the north where the weather beat unceasingly for 11 months of the year, all their dizzy heights alive with raucous birds. Then they were swept around a low headland, across a spit of sand and coral which made the water rough as it pushed the waves up to full height, and into a wide shallow bay.

"We'll beach here," said Slattery in an infinitely weary voice.

He brought the sturdy little boat round in a sharp curve and drove her up onto the beach. Then they killed the engine and sat for a moment in the silence, simply looking around. On their left, the shoulder of a hill rose into the darkening sky, seemingly clothed in sparse, short grass of some kind. On their right, a tail of land dwindled nakedly into the quiet sea. In front of them, the beach gathered itself lazily into a low dune or two, each sporting a light thatch of beach-grass. None of them dared even stand up to look further, for fear of what might be seen. Around them the waves hushed onto the sand. Far away the nesting birds screamed and squabbled. Above them, the wind whispered in the dune-grass.

Rebecca found that there were tears running down her cheeks. Then the wind veered a little and for a moment or two it blew over the island and right into their faces. And in those moments it carried with it a soft, infinitely beautiful tinkling sound. It was too light to be waves, too liquid to be anything other than water.

"Oh dear God!" breathed Rebecca, praying for all of them, "Dear God, let it be true!" They began to crawl unsteadily out of the boat, their movements made feverish by anxiety, hesitant by weakness, and unsteady by the unexpected steadiness of the land.

They went up off the beach, perhaps a hundred yards up a fairly steep slope and over a slight rise. The sound came and went in the shadows like a will o' the wisp to their ears, but it led them to their left, up the hill towards the distant cliffs. They followed it like sleepwalkers, stumbling but never falling. Shadows ahead became palm trees surrounded by low bushes, leaning in over the beautiful sound, nestling up against a low cliff, perhaps 20 ft high. Above, and a few yards behind it was another, smaller cliff. From the second cliff, across the shoulder of the first to a tiny hanging valley, and then down in a silver fall to a large pool among the bushes ran a tiny stream.

In a matter of moments they had thrust aside the bushes and fallen on their faces beside the water of the shallow pool. They drank like animals. They ran in to the icy, crystal water and splashed each other like children. They drank more. They laughed. They cried. They linked arms and danced in a rough circle in the water, kicking it up into brief rain. Then one by one they collapsed onto the grassy bank and watched those who still gambolled.

The pool was roughly circular. Two arms swept down on either side of the waterfall like stairways reaching to a balcony. These did not meet. Instead a broad, shallow valley showed where a rivulet must once have had enough force to run to the sea. On either side of this were low banks clear of trees which made an open space in the vegetation exactly opposite the waterfall.

After he had drunk and danced and laughed his fill, Stone began to gather dry palm-fronds and dead branches from the low bushes and lit a fire here. Slattery came and sat beside him; he seemed to have washed off years and a weight of worry with the salt and dirt in the pool.

"That's a good idea," he said. "They'll be a bit cold when they come out."

So they were, and hungry. They gathered, dripping, bedraggled but happy round the blaze. Wells went to the boat and returned with tins of corned beef and peaches. They roasted the tins of beef at the edge of the fire, and Stone produced a penknife with a broad, flat blade with which they scooped the hot meat into their suddenly watering mouths. "If only we had some coffee," said Mrs Gash. "If that had been an American ship, there would have been coffee." Everyone agreed, but nobody really cared.

They lay back on the soft ground and as the fire died the moon came up. The sky, visible through the gently-waving palms, was packed with stars. Fatigue washed over them with the gentle, idyllic sounds of the wind in the long fronds and the tiny, tinkling waterfall. One by one they slept.

With the dawn, the screaming of the birds on the cliffs became loud enough to wake them and the sky filled with the black shapes skimming, turning, riding the wind out to sea. Stone's eyes flicked open as soon as he woke, and he lay for a moment watching the birds. There came a quiet movement beside him. He did not move his head. Rebecca Dark rose into his field of vision, looked around without noticing that he was awake and began to unbutton the shirt she was wearing. Stone reluctantly closed his eyes. He heard the rustle as she shrugged the shirt off and her almost silent footsteps retreating on the short grass: towards the water, he thought. Then there was silence except for the birds.

And suddenly a terrible scream. Stone was up and halfway to the pool before anyone else moved. Then Gant was close behind him. And Wells. The shirt lay on the bank of the pool. Rebecca stood in the middle, almost up to her waist in water, her arms crossed over her breast. Stone had her trembling body pressed close and safe in his arms before he noticed that beside her, face down in the clear water, there was a body. He handed her to Eldridge Gant and gestured to Wells for help. Together they pulled the body to the far bank and turned it over.

Only amateurs cut a throat from ear to ear, for even with a very sharp knife it requires more than one slash to chop through the hard gristle of the windpipe before the carotid artery can be severed. A professional uses the point of the knife – which does not even have to be particularly sharp – and pushes it between the epiglottis and the muscle supporting the neck on the left side. This opens the carotid artery and if a hand is kept firmly on the victim's mouth for a very few seconds the desired effect may be attained with ease.

This is exactly how Slattery had died. The knife, still wedged between two of the neck vertebrae was the one with which Stone had served out the roast corned beef.

The two men sat back on their heels and looked at the corpse. It was totally colourless and only water oozed from the wound in Slattery's neck. Stone looked at Wells, who would not meet his eye. Instead, the blond reporter leaned forward to grasp the knife. Stone held his arm. Wells looked up. "We can't check for fingerprints here, you know," he said bitterly, a world of accusation darkening his voice. Stone frowned. The hairs on the back of his neck rose. The muscles of his back tensed of their own accord. He knew the feeling: it was fear. "Leave it for the moment, anyway," he said quietly.

"It's your knife," said Wells with a shrug: he might have been saying it's your life.

Gant came over. "My God!" He sat down unsteadily, his wet shirt bulging unevenly over the belt beneath it. "What do we do?" He was asking Wells, not Stone: he too had recognized the knife. Wells shrugged. Stone said nothing. "Where's the blood?" asked Gant. "He must have bled." Wells pointed to the pool. Gant nodded and shuddered. "What'll we do?" he asked.

"Nothing *to* do," said Wells. "We can't be certain who did it, after all."

"But the knife . . ." Gant still hadn't realized.

"Where did you leave it, Stone?" asked Wells wearily.

"In the ground by the fire."

"You see?" He turned to Gant once more. "It could have been any of us."

"If we ever get out of this," swore Gant, "I'll see the bastard fry."

"Perhaps," said Wells. Gant shook his head, almost in control of himself again. "Is there a spade?" he asked.

"God knows," said Wells, starting to get up.

"Take your knife, Stone," suggested Gant. The accusation was still there in his voice, dying but not yet dead. Stone worked the blade of his knife free of Slattery's cold neck, folded it and put it in his trousers' pocket. A shadow fell across them.

"Oh my God!" said Laughton. "Who did it?"

They all looked up at him. "Who knows?" said Wells. "Whoever it was used Stone's knife. That's all we know."

Laughton's eyes rested on Stone. "He was a good shipmate," he said. Stone looked up at him, eyes steady, saying nothing. Eventually Laughton looked away, and then turned away, his great square boxers' fists clenched and swinging like heavy weights.

Stone stood up unsteadily, legs stiff. The far side of the pool was empty. The shirt was gone. Rebecca must have gone back to the camp. Bates and Slobowski arrived and talked in low tones with Laughton. Then Stone read the message in their eyes also. The only way finally to prove his innocence would be to be murdered himself.

"We'll take care of him," said Laughton. He was speaking of Slattery but he might just as well have been talking about Stone. The three crewmen stood watching the three passengers over the dead man. Suspicion hung in the clear morning air like the threat of a terrible storm. Then Wells turned away. "Come on, Alec," he said. Stone followed him, and finally Gant followed Stone.

*   *   *

115

They buried Slattery just before midday and everyone was there. No spade had been found in the boat, nor anything to dig with and so they had taken the sail, wrapped the stiff body in it, packed the shapeless canvas bundle with stones and boulders and tied it like a bizarre parcel with rope from the rigging.

Behind the waterfall the island humped up quite steeply until it attained a small windswept plateau, perhaps 100 yards deep by 200 wide, bound on three sides by the cliff. At midday they all stood at the sheerest point of this plateau where the cliff fell more than 200 ft to the sea and to an untold depth beneath. Laughton said some words, but not many. His eyes kept straying to the passengers, wary and full of suspicion.

Stone stood a little apart, shunned by all, watching silently. "Until the sea shall give up her dead," said Laughton. It was as much as the boxer from Liverpool could remember of the marine burial service. Then Bates and Slobowski pushed the white canvas parcel off the cliff-edge. In silence, they all watched it falling.

It fell feet first until halfway down the cliff, where the rock took a slight step out and formed a ledge. The corpse bounced off the edge of this, sending up a shrieking cloud of birds and tumbled into the ocean. They stood until the pale, uncertain shape was lost in the fathomless blue and then they filed back to their camp by the pool.

"Well," said Gant eventually, over a moody silence. "I think we need a new leader."

"Why?" snapped Slobowski. He was angry and wary.

"Well . . ." Gant looked round for support. He felt it was imperative that there should be someone to make important decisions quickly: a leader.

"I agree," said Wells and Mrs Gash nodded brightly, very much a part of the conversation.

116

"Who, then?" asked Bates. He did not sound happy. His eyes kept stealing towards Slobowski and Laughton.

"I nominate Mr Gant," said Wells calmly, as though this were a board meeting of some civilised London club.

"I think Laughton," said Bates immediately, his eyes narrow and cunning.

"Yes," said Slobowski, backing Bates.

"I second Mr Gant," said Mrs Gash to put him in his place.

"We'll have to take a vote," suggested Wells.

"Bloody democracy," muttered Bates mutinously, but Laughton caught his eye and shook his head fractionally: he did not want to be the leader. He was far too well aware of what had happened to the last two who had held the post. Laughton and Gant did not vote of course. Bates and Slobowski voted for Laughton. Wells and the women voted for Gant.

Stone did not vote. Instead he wandered away, lost in a brown study. He still had a lot of thinking to do. There was quite a little forest on two sides of the pool and beyond the clearing where the river would run to the sea when the rains came. Beyond that, towards the low end of the island, there was open ground covered with grass which grew more and more sparsely until it led to a sandy ridge falling away on one side to a curve of low sand-cliffs and on the other to the bay where they had beached the boat.

Stone went down to the boat and then along the beach. As the island humped up again above him – he was walking back towards the cliffs – the crescent of sand narrowed until it seemed to vanish into the water, but here, with the waves busy about his feet, Stone discovered that he was at the point of a headland which fell back immediately into a second tiny bay bound entirely by low cliffs. He waded carefully round the headland and into the bay. It was shadowed and peaceful, the quiet broken only by birds, waves and wind. It was a perfect place to sit down, relax and try to work things out.

For weeks now, ever since he had, without warning or reason, been told to leave Singapore and was presented with a ticket for the next departing ship, he had known that someone – probably Nash – had put him back in the field. At first he had been angry, of course. They had no right and they knew it. He had served his time and been granted honourable discharge after Anne's death. But then he had thought: they will have known all that. Nash will have known it all and considered it all before sending his directive to those quiet, courteous policemen in Singapore. So the next logical question was: why? Why had they put him back in the firing line?

He took out his cigarette case: only five left, he would have to make them last. He lit one anyway, thinking. If Nash had put him here then there was a good reason. He had never particularly liked Nash, but he never underestimated him. And if there was a reason, then it had to have been important, because Nash – or whoever was responsible – had broken the rules. First of all he should have been officially recalled. That he had not been recalled at all did not really bother him. He would never lose the instinct for when an action was running: it was clearly unnecessary to drag him back to Queen Anne's Gate and say, "Look here old chap we've got a bit of an action running out of Singapore; we know you're retired and all that but would you mind *terribly* much . . ." It wasn't necessary, but it would have been courteous.

More important was the lack of equipment. He had never really enjoyed traipsing around the various scientific sub-sections stocking up like James Bond with all the latest gadgetry, home-grown and imported, but there was a great deal to be said in the most vicious of stress situations for the spiritual comfort a gun might bring. (This thought from a man who had always steered clear of guns in so far as he could.) Or a hyperpowerful microtransmitter with its built-in assurance that somebody out there cared for you, and might come in and save your bacon at any moment.

There was even some comfort to be derived from the old cyanide pills – at least you were among the elite with utter control over your own final destiny. But he had been dumped in at the deep end with no equipment, and he felt like a child who can swim perfectly well, but was missing his rubber ring.

Much more importantly, there was no Control. Nash had always been his Control during his working life. He had been one of the Soldier's stable. Soldier Nash. God! how it all came back. He hadn't thought of Nash or his nickname in years. How many others there had been working for Nash he never knew. He never wanted to know. Some agents, executives (another step back into the old slang) wanted to know all about their Control's other boys and girls.

An executive relied on his Control emotionally to a great extent, actually to the death sometimes. The bond between them was usually strong, even if they didn't like each other much. An executive needed a Control for myriad reasons. To hate when the going got rough. To blame when things went wrong and it would be fatal to blame yourself. To rely on when God wasn't listening to prayers. To make decisions when you didn't have time. To talk it all out with if you made it through. Stone had always been independent and self-reliant. He had never let Nash too close, or tried to get close to Nash. And yet now he was in the middle of an action without him, Stone suddenly felt alone and unprotected.

Finally and worst of all there had been no briefing. Stone found this enormously frustrating, and had he been more given to violence – like many others in his strange profession

119

– he would have taken it out in blood. Of course a briefing is necessarily a shadowy thing. It is like a play: a suspension of disbelief, a mutual unspoken agreement between those involved not to ask stupid questions but to take at face value a lot of stuff that in your heart of hearts you know is not quite real. Like an audience content to watch Hamlet die while knowing perfectly well that the actor playing him will rise again for a curtain-call, the executive listens to his Control's briefing or version of the current action complete with the agent's place in this action and his proposed actions and reactions, knowing perfectly well that on the ground it will all be entirely – perhaps fatally – different.

Nash had been superb at briefing. It was the heart of his success as a Control. Like a great dramatist, he would bring the action to life in his office in the Broadway Buildings. He would describe it in glowing technicolour, place you like Connery, Caine, Burton or Brosnan precisely in the middle, take you through what seemed like every permutation of possibilities, and explain to you how you could bring home the bacon yet again (and how *only* you could do it) to a country which would be infinitely grateful, if only they could know.

You knew and Nash knew that it wouldn't be like that, but he sold it to you every time, and it helped. It helped enormously, Stone now knew: for without it, without even the illusion that he knew what was going on, he found himself utterly out of his depth, and floundering around uselessly when he should have been swimming like a shark.

Still, without Control and Nash's technicolour briefing to guide him, he was still going to have to function. And, if necessary, that meant he would have to act as his own Control and brief himself. He shook his head. This was clearly enormously important, and not only to Nash. He thought about the bomb on the *Wanderer*. Who could have put it there? It was either political or it was private and commercial. He was tempted to rule out the latter because, although it was not unheard-of, SIS were usually too chary about the use of their executives to let them get mixed up in anything commercial – so his very presence here meant that it was almost certainly political. Who, then? The Russians? Had they a sufficient Far East network to arrange for a bomb on a British ship in the Singapore Roads? Probably.

Even in those times when everything was so different from the nice safe simple world he had worked in during the Eighties. They weren't even KGB any more. What did they call themselves now? FSS. That was it.

Or the Chinese? Almost certainly. Would either of them care about the scandal if they were caught? Perhaps.

And then Stone remembered that whoever it was probably didn't have to care because there were going to be no survivors to make a scandal. Well one survivor, perhaps, or two: the murderer and the person they seemed to be searching for. And these would only survive if they were found in time. But there would have to be checks. That was the only failing in what seemed to be an otherwise perfect plan.

If the ship was to be sunk with the agent on board, whichever power had started the action would have to be certain to pick up the survivors, or run the risk of a perhaps unwelcome scandal. Unless the agent, as seemed to be the case here, had been told to destroy the survivors himself or herself. In that case two possibilities existed: either this was a suicide mission – in this case unlikely for the murderer had had more than one chance to sink the lifeboat and destroy them all together – or the agent was searching for someone or something and was destroying witnesses who were not, or were not possessed of, what he or she was looking for.

In that case – in *this* case as that is what seems to be happening now – there must be somebody out there searching extremely carefully for their executive and whatever he is going to bring home with him. And even if he was not going home, ever – and in these circumstances that too seemed likely – the masters of this executive would have to be absolutely certain that he or she was dead. A shipwrecked agent, perhaps delirious, might be fatal in the wrong hands. No. In this sort of action, whoever planted the bomb that sank the *Wanderer*, whoever was running the executive who had killed Slattery, Spooner and probably O'Keefe, and who incidentally had punctured the cans and salted the water, whoever was responsible, would have to take the Indian Ocean to pieces and search it if necessary drop by drop.

Stone went back over his logic. It seemed good so far. The next two questions were Who? and Why? But the answers to these questions were tortuous and labyrinthine, leading his mind only to the cool quiet caverns of sleep. He was wakened some hours later by the explosion.

Gant decided that their first priority should be to explore the island fully. Bates and Slobowski showed every inclination to go off and leave them to it but Laughton managed to keep the peace and so they stayed for the time being. "I think," said Gant, "that we should split up. It will be quicker that way." The others nodded their agreement. "Well then, let's see: Miss Dark and I will follow the coast along from the boat towards the cliffs. Mrs Gash and Miss Buhl, perhaps you would like to go the opposite way from the boat down towards the point. The land seems quite flat down there, so you won't be put to any unnecessary exertion. Mr Laughton, perhaps you and Mr Bates could go up the cliffs from this side. Mr Slobowski, Mr Wells, there doesn't seem . . ."

"I want to go with Laughton and Bates," said Slobowski mutinously.

"And I think I'll just go and see what's happened to Stone," said Wells. And so it was decided.

It was just after 1400 when they all re-assembled at their makeshift camp by the pool. By that time they were in a good position to build up a fairly comprehensive picture of the island. It was almost two miles long, and at its widest point it was almost half a mile wide. From the sea it had looked like a wedge with sheer cliffs rising abruptly out of the water to slope gently back again into the low spit at its south-western end. From the air, however, it would resemble a rough comma.

At the top of the comma-shape were the cliffs. Facing India, these cliffs stood tall, curving round and falling away in a smooth curve of shore, until the cliffs of rock became cliffs of sand, then dunes, then the curling tail of the sand-spit. Facing Africa, however, the curve of the cliffs was much more abrupt. They came round almost in a semi-circle falling off much more rapidly until they formed the gentler slopes on the north side of the bay where the boat was beached. This bay continued to reverse the curve of the cliffs so that this coastline formed a huge letter 'S', the tail of the 'S' reaching out in the low sand-spit to join the reversed 'C' of the other coast at the low point of the sand-spit.

The main feature of the island was the stream they had found last night. It came out of the foot of a low cliff cut back into the steep shoulder of the slope climbing up towards the cliffs. It formed a small pool on a step in the rock, tumbled musically down the waterfall, formed a much larger pool on the thin soil at the foot of the second cliff, gave life to a few sage-like bushes and a couple of seemingly barren date palms on land, and a hoard of fascinating tiny silver-sided fish in its own clear heart, and then simply vanished.

There was none of the salt-pan edging which would have

123

suggested evaporation, so Gant, stretching his fourth-grade Physical Geography, reckoned it must simply be soaking into the rock. Away from the stream, the vegetation consisted mainly of a wild springy plant, seemingly a mixture of marsh-grass and heather. Here and there, more of the bedraggled bushes. Everything except the shaded riverside dwellers, was burned brown and sered by the sun.

The only non-plant life of the island except for the fish were the seabirds which nested in their thousands on the forbidding cliffs. They were black and raucous. They had reddish eyes and long, vicious beaks. Laughton said he thought they looked like gannets, but he didn't know enough about birds to be sure. "If the worst comes to the worst," said Gant, "at least we can eat them, if we can catch them; or their eggs, if there are any left this late in the year."

"Talking of eating . . ." said Slobowski, and began to get up. Wells sauntered into the clearing. "Any sign of Stone?" he asked.

"No," said Gant.

"That's funny. I couldn't find him anywhere. Never mind. I expect he'll turn up. Did someone mention food?"

"I'll get it," said Laughton, coming to his feet quicker than Slobowski.

"It's all right," said Wells to the Chicagoan, "I'm already on my feet. I'll help."

"Wells," said Gant as the little reporter turned away.

"Yes?" Wells turned back. "Hang on, Laughton," he called over his shoulder. Laughton paused. Gant looked around the rest of the group and then got up. Laughton began to walk towards the bay. Wells followed, with Gant catching him up. "Did you look everywhere for Stone?" he asked in a low voice.

"Everywhere I could think of. It felt quite creepy out

there on my own with him somewhere I didn't know about, I can tell you: even in broad daylight."

"You don't think he's been killed, then?"

"The thought never crossed my mind. No. I don't think Stone's going to die at all . . ." He left it at that and hurried after Laughton. Gant came to a stop at the top of the rise, looking down the dunes into the bay. Laughton strode purposefully across the beach towards the boat. Wells was hurrying to catch up with him. They seemed to be almost side by side when Laughton reached the boat. He called something to Wells and leaned over the gunwale. Wells hesitated fractionally, mopping his face with his hands and Gant found himself automatically echoing the action in the stifling heat. Then the boat blew up.

When it burst, Laughton was lifted on a livid balloon of fire and cast away like a blazing scarecrow. Wells was clear of the boat but close to the blast. He gave a strange ducking motion and the wave of red and black washed over him.

In a second he staggered clear but he too was ablaze now. Like a walking match in the mid-afternoon sun he staggered around the beach, making no sound, leaving a trail of heavy smoke. Then he turned and began to run towards the sea. Still burning he waded in.

Gant blasted forward like a sprinter then. "Lie down!" he screamed to the blazing Wells, but Wells couldn't hear. He continued to wade out into the water and he continued to burn. The others topped the rise above the beach. Gant hit the water, the first waves slapping viciously at his legs, his eyes riveted to the shapeless blazing bundle that was Wells. He could almost see the man behind the flames.

Then Wells slowly toppled forward. There was a loud hiss, a cloud of steam and he was gone. Gant reached the place the little man had fallen, but there was nothing except the stench of fire. He cast about in the water but there was

125

no sign of a body at all. The afternoon sun drew curtains of blazing gold across the surface and hid the depths. Once he thought he saw something, yards away towards the cliffs, but it was gone before he could clear his eyes.

With all the weight of the world on his shoulders he turned and waded ashore. The others were standing shocked, not knowing what to do. Laughton, yards away, was a crisp black homunculus, still burning. "How could this have happened?" whispered Gant, shaking his head.

Then Stone came running over the rise. Mrs Gash turned, screamed, "Him, he did it!" and pointed directly at Stone.

Stone took one look at the wreckage, the carnage and the almost insane faces, turned in a flurry of sand and began to run. Bates uttered a strange guttural sound somewhere between a sob and a cry. He launched himself after the fleeing man. Slobowski grabbed a length of oar, blazing at one end, from among the wreckage and followed Bates at full tilt. After a few yards Stone lost his footing in the soft sand and Bates was upon him, arms flailing wildly. Stone hardly seemed to move, yet the Radio Operator stumbled past without actually touching the fallen man. Then Slobowski arrived with 4 ft of smouldering oar.

"No!" cried Rebecca Dark.

Nobody seemed to hear her. Nobody moved. Stone lay on his back in the sand watching the smoking oar. Slobowski swung it at Stone's head: it brushed his shoulder. He drove it at Stone's belly: it whispered past his thigh. While it was part buried in the sand, Stone sprang easily to his feet. Slobowski tore it free and swung it at Stone's knees: it missed. Stone seemingly stood stock still and yet the oar could not touch him. Then Bates rejoined the attack.

They came from each side. Stone almost avoided them both but Slobowski caught his shoulder with the makeshift

126

club and he fell in a cloud of sparks. Bates swung a boot at the fallen man's belly and seemed to take off. Slobowski drove the oar at Stone's face but it was smashed away with the edge of a hand. Slobowski staggered back and Stone was on his feet. He stood easily, seemingly relaxed, breathing slowly through his nose. Bates came in with a knife, weaving like an expert. Stone rose onto the balls of his feet and stood with his arms at his sides, waiting.

"Do something! Please!" screamed Rebecca, but Gant just stood without moving.

Bates came in with the knife held wide and low, edge up, moving stiff-legged like a cat. He had all the confidence of a master and where at first he had been hot and wild he was now cold, precise and very deadly. Slobowski began to work his way quietly round behind Stone's back. Bates made a couple of quick passes, striking like a cobra, and Stone stepped back. Bates closed in again immediately, hissing, eyes narrow. Slobowski took another step forward, oar forgotten, arms wide. Bates struck once more. Stone swivelled from the hips but a 3 in gash opened in his shirtfront.

Rebecca screamed.

Slobowski dived forward and his arms closed around Stone's upper arms and chest. Bates ran forward, arm straight, the gleaming knife pointed unerringly at Stone's unprotected belly. His hiss of battle became a roar of victory.

And three things happened almost at once: Gant shot the knife from his hand; Slobowski gave a strangled scream and slumped back away from Stone; Stone caught Bates' still outstretched arm and hurled the stocky Radio Operator ten yards over the sand.

Then there was silence and stillness for a while. The wind picked up dry sand and carried grains of it onto their glistening skins. The grasses bowed and curtsied. Black smoke bellowed without noise away over the sea. Bates and Slobowski and Laughton lay where they had fallen. Miss Buhl clutched at Mrs Gash who looked lost and confused. Rebecca stood with her hands clutched into tight fists. Gant remained in police standard two-handed firing position – legs spread, back crouched, arms straight, gun ready at eye level still smoking. Stone stood gulping down great draughts of air, his face glistening, but calm and still as deadly as Bates' shattered knife-blade. Then he relaxed.

"Thanks," he said to Gant: but he was looking at Rebecca.

"Thanks for nothing," said Gant and put his gun away. Mrs Gash sagged silently to the sand.

"No, no! It's all right, really. Really," said Miss Buhl, crouching protectively over her employer and speaking over her shoulder to Rebecca. Rebecca shrugged and turned back to Stone. There was no accusation in her eyes, none at all. A tiny frown crossed Stone's face, too fast for her to see; but the frown remained as a question in his mind: Why doesn't she suspect me? He came up with four possible answers as she crossed the couple of yards of sand towards him.

First – she did it. Second – she knows who did it. Third – she likes me too much to admit the possibility that I did it. Fourth – she thinks I did it but still wants to side with me. He smiled at her.

"Did he cut you?" she asked, her finger on the slit in his shirt front.

"Yes." Her hair was oily, her face sprinkled with sand and freckles. She was peeling and she smelt strongly of sweat. She was utterly attractive to him.

"Oh!" she said. "Can I do anything for it? I did some

128

training as a nurse." He had never noticed before how velvet was her voice.

"It's not too bad. Just a scratch, as they say."

Her hands were warm and soft, "So it is. It's stopped bleeding already." She turned away. "Where did you learn to fight like that?" she asked.

"Me? I was not fighting."

"Well, where did you learn to *not fight* like that?"

He didn't answer because Bates and Slobowski were coming back, still bristling with suspicion. He wouldn't have told her about the farm near Stoke d'Abernon anyway.

"We want to get that murderous bastard out of the way," said Bates. Slobowski nodded. Gant shrugged: What could he do? "We have no proof," he said.

"Oh for Christ's sake," said Slobowski. "The old broad said she seen him. What more do you want?"

"I think that Mrs Gash," said Miss Buhl carefully, "was not quite herself when she accused Mr Stone."

"You know damn well she wasn't," said Rebecca, "She was out of her mind. And even if she had been okay, what right did that give the two of you, armed, to attack an unarmed man?"

"It is the most sensible way to do it," said Stone, mildly amused. "If you must attack someone, then do so with the minimum of risk."

"And that's what you were doing, I suppose, running like a buck-rabbit over that dune," said Slobowski, "Minimising risks!"

"Certainly," said Stone.

"Well you listen here, mother, that cuts no ice with me. I got you tagged for at least two homicides, and I am going to see you fry. If I don't get to you first."

"And me," said Bates. "There's another blade in that knife, so you'd better be bloody careful you don't wake

129

up one morning with it stuck in your throat like yours was in Slattery's."

"That's enough of that sort of talk, Bates," snapped Gant. The Radio Operator swung round, his face twisted with fury.

"And as for you, mister sharpshooting superstar, I don't take no orders from you. I don't trust you no farther than I can see you. I don't trust any of you." He turned and stalked angrily away, pausing only to pick up his broken knife. Slobowski looked around them with suspicious, narrowed eyes. "Yeah," he said, and followed Bates up the grassy slope.

"We'd better bury poor Laughton," said Gant wearily as the two figures began to labour up the steeper slopes in the distance.

"Hadn't we better see if there's anything we can salvage from the boat first?" asked Stone. But the fire was still burning too fiercely for them to go near it, so they buried Laughton first after all, digging in a sand dune with their hands. It was little enough, but it was all they could manage.

When the boat was cool enough for them to sift through the wreckage, there was precious little there. The diesel can was rounded and burst open. The Very pistol was twisted and burned. Apart from the blackened ribs of the boat still sticking out of the fire-blackened sand, all that remained relatively untouched were a few cans thrown yards away by the power of the explosion.

Miss Buhl wouldn't let any of them near Mrs Gash. She had covered the older woman's head and supported her over the 100 yards or so to the shady pool. Here she had laid her down by the water and had started to bathe her face while the others were burying Laughton. Mindlessly, she was still doing so when they came back with their pitiful store of tins from the wreckage. "Is there anything . . ." asked Rebecca solicitously.

"No. No, really. She'll be all right if she can just rest. She's very strong, you know, but the last few days . . . They've . . . Well, they've been a bit of a strain. It's the heat, I expect; that, and . . ." She made a vague gesture with her hand towards the distant boat.

"I'd better say a few words for poor Wells, too," said Gant in a low voice to Stone. "No hope of finding his body now, of course. Not that there would be all that much to find." Stone nodded, saying nothing.

"God *damn*! What a business!" exploded Gant after a second. "It's no wonder Mrs Gash has collapsed. Nor that those other two don't trust us. I don't know who to trust myself. I certainly don't trust you."

Stone grinned mirthlessly: "Nor I you."

They looked sombrely down at the three women. "Still," continued Gant. "We're both actors . . ."

"Of one sort or another," agreed Stone. And they went down to the beach together.

The tropical night came suddenly and the four of them had corned beef from their diminishing supply, saving Mrs Gash's share until she should recover. The two sailors had taken a little. There was enough for perhaps two more days. Gant and Stone thought about setting watch but ultimately decided that it would be useless. They lit a fire and all agreed that should anyone waken for whatever reason during the night, he or she should add a few more branches to keep it going. Then they all went to sleep. It had been a long day and they slept soundly.

A little after midnight Miss Buhl woke slowly. She tossed and turned a little, then stood up. She dutifully piled some more sticks on the fire and Stone woke up as the embers

131

blazed. Miss Buhl nodded cheerfully at him, checked that Mrs Gash was all right and crept silently into the brush.

Stone watched her go, thinking, "I'd better stay awake until she comes back." But his mind became involved in the mechanics of making an extremely powerful little bomb out of the odds and ends they had left in the boat. The process of making this bomb drew out tediously and infinitely until Stone was sound asleep.

The day arrived as abruptly as had the night. Alec Stone rolled over, his mind still full of bombs and booby traps. He looked at the distant blue of the sky still with its traces of dawn-grey like fine smoke. The palms rustled high, moved by a wind which only came fitfully to the ground. A little dust-devil danced out of a shadow and died almost immediately by Miss Buhl's bed. Stone watched it idly. It spread a fine patina of sand over the coat Miss Buhl slept on, covering the bright Burberry-pattern lining with minute grains of dust. Another breath of wind came. The coat stirred and flapped a little, clearing the dust away. Stone turned over, wriggling hips and shoulder into the springy earth. The waterfall curved over the hard edge of the little cliff, its tinkling murmur calling him back to sleep.

And then he realized Miss Buhl was not there.

Sleep vanished from his mind like the grey from the sky. He rolled onto his feet with one fluid motion. He looked swiftly around the camp, his eyes flicking over the sleeping forms: Mrs Gash, Rebecca, Gant. His head turned from side to side. He had seen her leave. Where had she gone? Where? Into the brush. He went over to her bed and looked for something to show him which way she had gone: some sort of a trail. There was none.

He returned to his own resting-place and looked towards

the fire trying to reconstruct last night's scene now in his memory. There! he thought. She had gone through there.

Stone followed. A small sandy clearing in the low scrub which was their improvised latrine. Beyond that only a small rise and a slope down to the sea. There was nothing here: nothing and nobody. He looked for tracks in the sand of the clearing, on the dunes, on the beach. Nothing. He returned to the latrine and stood there with his mind racing. The wind whispered knowingly. The waterfall sang. The slow surf rumbled like an earthquake on the beach. Seagulls screamed incessantly as though horrified. He knew it would do no good but he called out, "Miss Buhl?" No answer.

Skin like ice, he turned and went back to camp. Twice on the way he stopped suddenly and swung round as though he expected someone to be stealing along silently just behind him.

They were all still asleep. He hated to wake them. From his very soul he hated the idea of their confusion, anger and pain. He collapsed onto the ground glowering. The black lines of his eyebrows joined above his nose. "You were born to be hanged with eyebrows like those," his grandmother used to tell him as a child. "You may become a sailor and go to sea for you will never drown you know. You were born to be hanged, young man." He sat straight-backed with knees apart and calves crossed like a red Indian at a pow-wow. His big hands joined, the right grasping the left, forearms resting on kneecaps. His face became utterly still. The deadly stillness of the knife blade settled on his features. His mind broke free.

Who?

Why?

God damn Nash: God damn you Nash. I am an executive and you are expecting me to work like an administrator.

You know how I work: I get an assignment, I am provided with cover and some sort of a plan. I prepare, I run, I execute.

I have a Control: I need a Control.

I need someone who can think logically and clearly no matter what is going on. Someone who can weigh alternatives and dismiss improbabilities. Someone to take the decisions and carry the can. Who can tell me what to do and look after the grieving relatives. God! Look at me! Hands and arms trembling. My knees will be knocking next. What sort of an Action is this anyway? God, Dear God but I hate you Nash!

"Hate me all you want to, Stone, but hate those bastards more." That was Nash, London, years ago. He had been a good Control. They say he's an Administrator now. A non-active Administrator.

Executive: Control: Administrator.

That was the ladder Nash had climbed, the ladder Stone had been climbing all those years ago. Hate me all you want but hate those bastards more. Good old Soldier. The perfect motto for the perfect Control. You were right, Nash. You were right. Executives hate where they need to, love where they need to, manufacture any emotion they need to get the job done. Controls have no emotion: they have thought, logic, psychology, reason. Administrators have information.

An Administrator knows a certain Cabinet Minister is selling secrets where he shouldn't: he says to a Control: "Minister X needs to be terminated." Control says to an Executive: "You will go to Westminster, tomorrow at ten, in a black car with CD number plates. When you see the man in this photograph crossing the road, you will run him down and kill him." And that is what the Executive does. A theoretical case. An illustration. Administrator,

134

Control, Executive: Information, Thought, Action. That is what makes each what he is: their being and their reason for being.

Stone continued to stare at nothing, but his hands had come to rest. He got up slowly but without hesitation and went over to Gant. "Mr Gant, wake up." He shook the American actor's shoulder gently and Gant woke up.

"Miss Buhl is gone," he said. Gant sat up. Stone rocked back on his heels and watched Gant begin to assimilate the fact. All the panic was gone from his mind. He stopped thinking for a moment and simply observed – as though he were trying to get inside the role of Sherlock Holmes or Poirot for the stage. Even when he got up and went to help Gant look in places he had already looked he kept his mind utterly quiet until, almost unbidden, memories, observations, old and new of the island, the boat, the ship came into his mind and instead of begetting emotions they begat reasoned patterns.

And Stone had become his own Control.

". . . the sailors. It must be those two sailors," said Gant. There was a silence and then he said, "She's just not here, Alec."

"No."

"God *damn*! I don't understand any of this. It's the work of some kind of maniac. It has to be." I've been this kind of maniac, thought Stone, and I think you have too, at one time or another. He shrugged.

"We'd better organize a proper search party and check with Slobowski and Bates." Stone nodded his agreement, mind elsewhere. *Who?* The question nagged. He had no answer, of course, so he reluctantly put it out of his mind for the time being. The question served no purpose at the moment: its time would come. And its answer.

They went back to the camp. The two women were still

135

sleeping. Gant stood helpless, so Stone woke them. "Miss Buhl's gone," he said.

"Oh God!" said Rebecca, understanding immediately.

"Gone where?" enquired Mrs Gash vaguely. "I do hope she'll be back soon. I'm lost without her, you know. Gone where?"

"Gone: vanished," said Stone. "Gone: disappeared. Most likely dead."

His eyes rested on her narrowly. Her face slowly sagged. It became blurred, doughy, fat, old. Her chin clenched and became pitted. Her bottom lip trembled. Her eyes filled. She turned her head away like a hurt child.

"You BASTARD!" screeched Rebecca.

Stone got up. No one was more aware than he how completely emotions could be represented by a competent actor, but it seemed that Mrs Gash's reaction to his measured cruelty had been just too perfect not to be real. His voice became deep, soothing and very gentle. "We still need to look," he told her, "just in case she's wandered off after all."

"Oh yes," said Mrs Gash, "she might have done that. We must go and look." Her face brightened as she climbed to her feet and she walked away calling, "Letty? Letty!" quite cheerfully. Rebecca followed her. She did not look at Stone. After a moment, the two men followed.

They began their search at the narrow end of the island and, as well as they were able, covered all the ground between that narrow sandbar and the bird-loud cliffs at the other end. Here they found Slobowski and Bates crouched by a small fire roasting the inevitable corned beef.

"What do you want?" demanded Slobowski in a surly voice. Bates drew closer to his shoulder, they both protected their little cache of food with their bodies like animals.

"We've lost Miss Buhl," Gant explained.

Mrs Gash began to babble, "You have seen her, haven't you? Sometime during the night. You have. I know. Oh do say you have! Please." She was verging on the incoherent again. The fruitless search up the length of the island had crushed her spirit even more than the initial discovery had. Slobowski shook his head.

"Sorry, lady," he said. He even looked sorry. There was a silence. "Look, lady," said the big American after a while, "I tell you what we'll do. We'll help you look. She was a nice little broad; full of spunk. It'd be a right shame if anything had happened to her. Who saw her last?"

"I did," Stone said, and watched the suspicion deepen in their eyes. Slobowski nodded as though he had expected nothing less, but all he said was, "Where?"

"At the camp, late last night. I supposed she was going to relieve herself."

"Yeah, that sounds just like her, waiting until everybody was asleep before going to pay a call."

"Why didn't you raise the alarm when she didn't come back?" asked Bates, his voice dripping with accusation.

"I went back to sleep."

"Convenient!" he sneered, but Stone let it rest.

"Any tracks? Sign of a struggle?" asked Slobowski. Stone wondered whether he was just naturally a clear thinker or whether he had been trained to think like that. He said, "No. None."

"She would have left tracks going to the john. Someone must've wiped them out."

Gant nodded – "He'd have had to do it to the edge of the brush. Beyond that the grass is pretty thick. And the sand is pretty well churned up anyway."

"O.K. But why bother?"

Silence: Nobody had thought of asking why.

137

"Because he didn't want us to know where he was coming from?" Rebecca, uncertain.

"Or who he was?" Gant.

"How could tracks tell us who he is?" sneered Bates.

Stone looked around them. "They would tell us quickly enough if 'he' were a she."

Rebecca swung towards him, mouth open. Mrs Gash gobbled, her eyes round. "Or," he continued relentlessly, "if there were no 'he' at all and Miss Buhl simply wanted to disappear." They all thought about that.

"Well, we'd better look again, all the same," said Slobowski, unimpressed by this display of logical reasoning.

They returned to the camp and began another, more thorough, search. The extra eyes made no difference: there was still no sign of Miss Buhl. The morning wore on through to afternoon, and they ran out of places to search. The beach where the black skeleton of the boat lay was empty except for Laughton's grave. The sandbar has still except for the blowing sand. The blackstone cliffs were alive only with the birds. The cove above the beach peopled only with the echoes of their cries.

At last they returned to the clifftops where the sailors had spent the night. The fire was dead now. Bates re-lit it and they settled down to eat something. During the day the sailors' mistrust had faded, and the necessity of working together to try to protect everyone had been borne upon them. "We haven't got much up here," said Slobowski apologetically.

"We didn't take no more than our fair share," said Bates defensively, running a hand through his light brown hair.

"That's O.K." said Gant expansively. Mrs Gash had been silent all through the afternoon. After the food she retired behind a convenient bush.

138

The sky was beginning to darken. Gant looked up at the spiralling birds. "There should be eggs down there," he said, wandering to the cliff edge. "They'll be a nice change from that corned beef if we can get at them."

"We brought some rope out of the boat before it blew up," said Slobowski. "We could lower somebody over to see."

"We've brought the rope up with us. We've got it here," said Bates. He turned to the pile of their supplies, and as he did so there was a terrible scream.

"What's that?" snapped Gant.

"Mrs Gash!" Rebecca.

"Mrs Gash?" Stone, on his feet. "Mrs Gash?" The scream went on and on. They ran into the gathering gloom. Stone caught up a blazing branch from the fire. Behind a bush a little way from the camp stood Mrs Gash alternately screaming and choking for breath.

Before her, neatly folded on the ground, lay all of Miss Letty Buhl's clothes.

Rebecca and Stone supported Mrs Gash back to their camp. Gant followed. Nobody had anything to say to Bates or Slobowski who yelled after their retreating figures, "We don't know nothing. Honest to God!"

That night they kept watch from the moment they began to feel sleepy, long before sunset. Stone and Gant took three hours each, then Rebecca took two, cradling Gant's snub-nosed .38 revolver beside the blazing fire, then Stone again and Gant until dawn. Nothing happened. Stone sat through the long weary hours thinking fruitlessly. When Gant took over he went to sleep thankfully. In the early hours Rebecca woke him: "Your turn again."

"Great. Thanks." The sleep had refreshed him, cleared his mind. He built up the fire and moved closer to its bright blaze. Shadows danced like witches round the edges of the clearing, now hiding, now revealing the three restless sleepers in a beguiling display of magic. The song of the waterfall almost drowned the subliminal earthquake rumble of the surf and the restless whispering of the wind in palm fronds, bushes and grass. After a while he pulled a stick from the bundle of firewood, smoothed the sand at his feet and like a geometrician began to examine a problem.

He drew a rudimentary boat-shape. Down the middle he drew a straight line. Down this line he drew eleven circles, and a twelfth a little away between the end of the line and the stern of the boat. By the eleven circles he drew the letters G D S S L O W B G B S. Each letter represented a name: each circle a person. The line down the boat was the oar and the twelfth circle was Spooner. That was the problem: How?

On one of his courses a small, bald man with pebble glasses had explained at length about bombs and how to detonate them. "Now this detonator has a rocker mechanism. It is a kind of trembler switch which reacts to any movement. The rocker mechanism works on the same basic principle as a see-saw. It is basically controlled by the fulcrum, where it is balanced. All the forces which act upon the mechanism are centred here. The switch itself is balanced flat on the fulcrum, like the board on a see-saw. If the mechanism is subjected to any movement, the state of equilibrium is upset and one end or other of the see-saw sinks – thus making contact and Bang!"

Stone was nodding and digging the stick deep into the sand as though stabbing the earth.

"What are you doing?" He didn't hear. Rebecca rolled over in her shadowed bed and asked again. This time he heard her, "Looking at a bomb," he said.

She sat up and pulled her tangled hair back behind her right ear. The firelight flared. The shadows magically danced away. Brightness played on her long body. The shirt she was wearing had come undone but she seemed to be unaware of it. Stone's glance lingered momentarily upon her breasts nestling in the shadow. She pulled the shirt closed and tugged it down over her long tawny thighs.

"I couldn't sleep," she said. He nodded, scrubbing the drawing out. "Do you really think that it is one of those sailors who has been doing all this?" He thought of his diagram. "They're both possibles," he told her. She shivered. "So am I," he added.

Now why had he said that? He frowned. After years of hiding everything from Anne, his wife who had left him and died, he was now making a game of doing the opposite with this strong, appealing woman.

She sat back and watched him. What is he thinking about behind that fierce scowl, she wondered. Why had he said that about himself? Was he trying to warn her that he was really the murderer? She did not doubt, looking at him, that he could kill.

And when that calm, cold look settled on him during the fight with Bates and Slobowski, she thought that perhaps he had killed. And what was he? An actor. A fine actor by all accounts. Looking at him she could see Richard III without the devilish, self-destructive humour. Not Hamlet, but Claudius, Hamlet's uncle, the tortured King. Macbeth: yes. Macbeth certainly, finding strength in doing evil. Only, of course, such figures did not exist in real life.

She shivered suddenly. This was a face of Stone she had not seen before and it might very well be the face of a killer. She shifted uneasily, remembering how easily he had taken the two sailors. But when he looked up, although his eyes were still cold and distant, he was smiling slightly.

"Have you been with Mr Gant long?" he asked.

141

"Some time. It's great fun I must admit. We go all over the world, you know. First Class." She smiled like a child showing off a treasure. Stone smiled back. "And I get to see all his great performances. We're going to do *Long Day's Journey Into Night* next. His James Tyrone is going to be better than Olivier's."

"Stone's smile became indulgent: he shook his head. "No," he said.

"Well, . . ." she tilted her head a little, aware that she had been a little outrageous, "different, then."

"I must come and see it."

"Oh yes, do. Unless . . . well, it hasn't, . . ."

"Hasn't what?"

"Hasn't been cast yet."

"You think I should try for Jaimie? It's the lead."

"Someone has to play it." She swept another few strands of hair back behind her ear.

"Don't," said Stone, so she left it. She looked up at him.

"It's all tangled," she said. "I must try to wash it tomorrow, too." Stone smiled. "What is it?" she asked.

"I was just thinking that neither on Treasure Island nor on the Coral Island did anyone ever seem to wash. Robinson Crusoe probably did, but I can't remember."

"People don't in books. You know that. Well, not in that sort of book. It's like at the beginning of *Swallows and Amazons* or whatever, where it says that we're just getting the exciting bits and we're to imagine people doing boring things like getting washed and having tea without being told."

"Was that in *Swallows and Amazons*? I don't remember."

"I'm not sure. It's a long time since I read it."

"It's a day or two since I did, too, I must admit. What were we talking about?"

"My hair."

He nodded. A silence came and lingered. Rebecca looked at him from under lowered lashes. His eyes fell on the jumbled mess of his drawing in the sandy dust. The look she didn't understand, like or trust settled on his face once more. The fire spluttered. The waterfall fell into the pool. They both glanced up one last time as though of one accord.

Their eyes met. She did not reach for him nor he for her. After a while she lay down and went back to sleep.

Stone drew the boat again, and the oar, and the circles, but his mind was too restless to extract more than the obvious from it. Perhaps there was no more. Rebecca stirred. The shirt fell open all down her body. Stone looked at her long and hard, bitterly regretting his inaction.

At just after 0400 on the morning of 22 July, Stone woke Gant and went back to sleep again. He awoke nearly ten hours later. Gant was asleep behind him and Mrs Gash beyond Gant.

Rebecca was not there.

Stone came to his feet immediately, his skin ice-cold and crawling, and looked around the clearing. At first he did not see her but she was there, crouched in the dappled shade beyond the pool. In cold water and without the aid of soap, she was washing her hair. For a moment he watched. She knelt, unaware of his scrutiny, wearing only her now grubby white panties, her hair a gleaming black cascade around her. Stone moved silently back to his sleeping place and lay down. After a while he heard her coming back. He stirred as though waking and smiled gently at the muffled exclamation and the covert rustle as she covered her nakedness. He yawned ostentatiously, opened his eyes, winced at the light, stretched, scratched, yawned again and climbed stiffly to his feet.

"Morning," said Rebecca brightly. She had washed her

shirt as well as her hair. Stone suddenly became aware that he stood in urgent need of a wash himself. He smiled at Rebecca. "Morning," he said, and he might have said more but Mrs Gash woke then and began to cry. Rebecca went to comfort her. Stone went to the pool, stripped off his shirt and trousers, waded into the cold, clear water and washed himself.

It was that afternoon, as much to occupy Mrs Gash as for any great danger of sunstroke – though they were all suffering from the fury of the sun – that Gant suggested that the women should make palm-frond hats. While they were doing so, the men wandered off. After a while they split up, not for any reason but because they each wanted to be alone. Mrs Gash wandered off too, when she had finished her hat and then Rebecca also left the glade.

The sun was low in the sky when they all drifted back into their camp. They came in as they had left: singly. Mrs Gash came in first, vague and lost. Every now and then she would look behind her as though expecting to see Miss Buhl in her usual place three paces back. She found the clearing by chance, and lingered like a child, fascinated by the waterfall. Rebecca found her there, and they sat side by side without speaking. Then Gant returned, hot and weary. He lay on his stomach by the pool and plunged his head into the cold water. For a moment the only sound was that made by the actor drinking his full.

But then in the distance there came a strange undulating scream which flew closer and closer until Slobowski, his mouth wide, his face swollen, purple and mad, burst into the camp.

"You . . .! you . . .!" he screamed. "Which of you? You!" And he went for Gant. Gant was on his knees by the water, but he had turned towards the big American. Slobowski took a short shambling run towards him and aimed a

144

massive kick at his head. Gant threw himself sideways, rolled under Slobowski's heavy seaboot and grabbed the other ankle unsteady on the sand. He twisted it with all his wiry strength, causing the solid Pole to fall. Gant was up like a cat, aiming a short sharp kick of his own at Slobowski's head. It connected with a dull thud and the fight was over as suddenly as it had begun.

"Now what was all that about?" asked Stone. He was sitting on a rock outcrop at the head of the waterfall, looking down at them like Puck in *A Midsummer Night's Dream*. Nobody answered, so he shrugged and began to run lightly down the curving slope from the top of the cliff to the clearing. Gant rolled Slobowski's inert body over towards the pool and pushed his face into the water.

By the time Stone joined them, Slobowski was coughing and spluttering, and trying to sit up. Gant helped him. In a moment he had shaken the confusion from his mind and was glowering at them all. "I don't trust you. None of you!" he said violently. They said nothing. He tried to get up. – Gant stopped him. "What happened?" asked Rebecca gently. Slobowski sat in moody silence. "This is silly, Mr Slobowski," she said. "Please tell us." So he shrugged and told them.

At lunchtime Bates and he had finished what little was left of their corned beef and had still felt hungry. Slobowski, himself, had remembered what Gant or Stone had said about the gulls' eggs on the cliffs and they decided that Bates should go down for them. Slobowski, being by far the heavier and stronger, would hold the rope. So Bates had knotted one end securely around his waist and the big Chicago Pole had lowered him gently over the cliff edge. In order to gain safe purchase with his feet, Slobowski had stood well back from the cliff edge and so he couldn't see Bates going down, but they had

145

kept up a steady flow of conversation. "You all right, Bates?"

"Fine. Give us more rope."

"See any eggs?"

"Not here. Farther down . . . Christ!"

"What is it?"

"It's a hell of a long drop down here."

"You want I should pull you up?"

"Nope. More rope . . . that's it. Got one. Hope they're allright. Shoo off old lady. And another."

"Mind them birds, Bates. I heard tell they'll maybe attack guys going after their eggs."

"Fine time to tell me that."

"Yeah. Sorry." They were yelling now, to make themselves heard above the screaming of the birds.

"No trouble. Bit more rope."

"There ain't too much left up here."

"OK. Won't be long. Hang on as they say. Hey!"

"What!"

"Give us another couple of feet would you? There's a sort of a ledge down here. There. That's it." The strain went off the rope. There was a silence. It lengthened.

"Bates, you still there?"

"'Course I am. You can let go now, sit down. Have a rest."

"You sure?"

"Yeah. 'Course. There's a ledge down here maybe a yard wide with a sort of a hollow going back into the cliff. It's really snug."

"Slobowski sat down, wedged the rope under his foot and relaxed. "How many eggs you got?" he yelled after a while.

"Five. I . . ." Silence from Bates. Sudden. The voice stopping abruptly as though his head had been cut off. Slobowski sat upright.

146

"Bates? What is it, Bates?" Silence: he couldn't believe it.

"Aw, come on Bates, stop messin' around. Bates, you there?" As he asked, he had started to get up and suddenly the end of the rope whipped out from under his foot. He grabbed at it. Missed. The end brushed his fingers and vanished over the cliff as he screamed, "BATES!"

That night Slobowski ate with them but after the food was done he wandered off on his own into the dark. Stone, Rebecca and Eldridge Gant kept watch as they had the night before beside the hissing fire: Stone, then Gant, then Rebecca for two hours, then: "Wake up, Alec!" Quiet voice. The gentle hand on his shoulder. Stone stirred. "Alec. It's your turn." Stone woke. Rebecca was beside him, her hair like a curtain of shadow. He moved languorously. His hand brushed the cool column of her thigh. She moved, flinched like a startled deer, and yet remained. "Are you awake," she whispered.

"Yes."

Silence. Stillness. Then her hair closed about him – wings of the night. As they kissed, she moved her body, extending her legs until she was pressing her whole length against him. He slid his thigh between hers and she moved against it. His body stilled as their lips parted.

"Yes," she whispered. "Oh, yes." His hands at her shoulders pushing the shirt away. Her hands at the waist of his trousers. His hands under the web of her hair high on her shoulders: her hands at his shoulders pushing the shirt away. The fire chuckled. The wind in the palms whispered. The sea rumbled. The waterfall sang. A single bird, black and cruciform against the enormous moon, let fall its raucous cry like a leaf in an English autumn.

147

The lovers paused. Lingered. Explored. His lips at her throat. Burning. His tongue gathering salt drops at the pit of her throat. Her back arching above him. Her head raised suddenly, thrown back, her lips parted and dumb. Her eyes wide and blind.

His hands at her waist pushing down: her hands at his echoing the action. Her face at the junction of his neck and shoulder, her leg thrown over his loins. His hands low on her back moving down. Her skin like satin fire under his fingertips.

"Yes! Oh yes," she whispered. Convulsively he bucked her over until their positions were reversed upon the massive springy mattress of the turf.

They did not wake Gant when his time came to keep watch. They made love until dawn.

Then they dressed.

Then they slept.

"You didn't wake me," said Gant to Stone.

"No," said Stone. Gant knew then but said nothing. It was late morning. Stone had just woken. They were alone. "I thought it would help morale if we built a watch fire up on the cliff top where Slobowski and Bates were, and kept watch there. In case of rescue," said Gant. "We built it this morning while you were asleep."

"You should have woken me."

"No need. There wasn't all that much to build a fire with anyway and none of it was heavy."

"No."

"Rebecca and Mrs Gash are up there now. I thought it would help morale."

"I'm sure it will." Stone got up and went to the pool. He

began to sluice his face. Gant stood by his shoulder. "You and Rebecca, are you serious?"

"Serious enough." Stone's tone of voice asked what business was it of Gant's, anyway?

"I've always thought of myself as being *in loco parentis* with regard to Rebecca."

"Yes?"

"I don't want to see her hurt."

"I won't hurt her."

"No." There was a dead fall to Gant's voice. And they let the subject rest.

After a while Gant went off to check on the women by the watch fire. Stone remained by the pool, deep in thought. Then he roused himself, climbed to his feet, looked around the glade and went through the bushes to the place where Miss Buhl had disappeared. Here he stood for a moment and then he moved purposefully up the slope towards the head of the waterfall. As the slope steepened he began to leave tracks in the soft earth. On this side the bushes thickened, and there was a path, so vague as to be invisible to anyone who was not following it with a good degree of certainty. Yet someone had been this way, and more than once.

Stone followed this as the slope eased off until the bushes suddenly gave onto a small clearing. There was a small cliff on Stone's left, a little over 10 ft high. Above and beyond it the ground began to hump up steeply in the final climb towards the cliffs. At the foot of the cliff a pool reached across the little clearing, narrowed in a funnel of rock and tumbled away into the waterfall which 20 ft below would give birth to the pool beside which stood their camp.

Stone glanced around the clearing, he looked up the bush-covered cliff and then stepped carefully into the small pool. The water came up to his knees. He waded forward until he reached the place where the water came out of the rock. At the very foot of the cliff there was a small cavern perhaps 4 ft high. Stone got out his silver cigarette-lighter, lit it, turned the gas up until the flame was as high as it would go, and ducked into the little cavern.

At first he could see nothing and was aware only of the sudden cold. When his eyes grew more used to the darkness, however, Stone saw that he was in a narrow, low-ceilinged passage which seemed to lead back into the heart of the hill. There was a slight movement of air, and the current against his legs was surprisingly strong. Shading the flame of his cigarette-lighter with his left hand, he bent his head and stooped his shoulders well clear of the roof of the tunnel and followed it on in as silently as he could. The flame in his hand danced in a slight silent draught, making the black, glistening walls dance and heave around him like monstrous waves breaking over his head.

The stream grew deeper, its cold surface creeping up his thighs and past his waist. When the water had risen until it was under his arms, Stone put his lighter out for fear he might slip, drop it and lose it. He put it in his shirt pocket, closed and safe even under water, and waded on with hardly a pause.

Suddenly something struck him on the head with unexpected, devastating force. He threw himself backwards, rolling with the blow, hands outstretched and hooked, feeling for his adversary, feet kicking in the water as he tried to regain his balance. His shoes twisted and skidded on the stream bed, but after a moment he managed to heave his head out of the water and he stood silently waiting for a sound from his attacker. Nothing.

He opened his mouth to its fullest extent, gulping in great silent draughts of air, preparing his body for the exertion of the next attack. Nothing. Stone moved his feet inch by inch and his body without sound through the water, circling upstream, arms outspread, fingers grasping only the cold dark. Still nothing.

Then, as suddenly as before, an agonising blow to his left ear. He rolled away from it again but this time he did not lose his balance. He swung round at once and moved in, his arms full outstretched in the utter blackness. After a few steps his hands encountered a solid rock wall. They followed it down to just a few inches above the water. It blocked the tunnel completely.

Stone smiled: so this was his mysterious, silent attacker.

Moving in the dark and colliding with it, he had automatically assumed he was being struck.

Stone bent his knees until his nose was just above the surface and then proceeded carefully forward. The roof of the tunnel remained a few inches above his head, invisible but pressing down in the dark like a multitude of hands all trying to force him under the water to drown. Using hands and arms outstretched like a tightrope walker to steady himself he moved slowly forward trying to control the claustrophobia which bore down upon him with the phantom hands and the invisible roof, until suddenly his right foot slipped and the water grasped his throat, cascading down his nose. His hands, waving wildly above the surface of the water grasped only the air. It was a second before Stone realized that the rock roof was no longer just above his head. He regained his footing and stood up choking and gasping for breath, no longer caring how much noise he made.

When he had steadied himself, Stone stood still and looked around. As his eyes probed the darkness, vague shapes began to form: light and shadow, far and near. Pointed towers, dark icicles of rock; perfect here and there but mostly broken and rotten. Stalactites and stalacmites. They looked like the teeth of some huge sea-monster. Stone knew what Jonah must have felt like and he shivered.

151

It was a moment before it occurred to him that if he could see then there must be light coming from somewhere. Enough light to give a certain amount of brightness right throughout what seemed to be an enormous cave. He began to look around first, therefore, for the source of this light. It was in the roof, high above him. So high that Stone suddenly realized that the whole hill at the cliff-end of the island must be hollow.

He pressed on, certain that any noise he made would be covered by the incessant tinkling hubbub of water in the great cave. He made for the side of the pool and sat on the cold, slippery floor to regain his breath and get his bearings. Assuming he had been following a straight line along the stream, he was now some little way behind the cliff from which the stream issued. And from the look of it, the cliffs would be far off on his right. He walked across the huge cathedral-like cave, staggered by the simple size of it.

How large it was Stone could not have begun to estimate. It was certainly more than 100 ft high. It seemed to have a floor area of more than a square mile. He knew something about caves in limestone country all over the world which had grown to incredible size, but this was far larger than any he had heard of. He could not see the walls, only the forest of stalacmites and stalactites like a jumbled set of columns all around. The floor was running with water.

Much of it was plain rock, flat and slick, but there were areas of pebbles, stones and even a few boulders. It sloped slightly towards the pool so that all the water from the walls ran down and collected there. He walked on, half expecting to come to a gallery of still more massive proportions immediately behind the cliffs, but instead the ceiling swooped down to meet the floor far back from where he judged the shoreline to be. He walked the line of this wall until he came to the mouth of another tunnel.

This tunnel was dry, but utterly dark. Over the sound of the cascading water, however, he heard distant screams echoing up the throat of the rock. Store began to follow the dry tunnel, groping like a blind man. The screams grew louder with each step he took and he began to hurry. A foul smell suddenly burned in the back of his throat. He began almost to run. Another, smaller, tunnel entrance on his right echoed with the screams. He stumbled on, gripped by the terrible agony of the sound.

Such was his concern that he made a mistake – he rounded a tight bend without thinking and was struck blind by the light. He put his hand up over his streaming eyes and stood rooted. The screaming was solid around him. It beat in his quaking mind. The acrid smell tore at his lungs as the water had done. He leaned against the nearest wall and forced his eyes open.

Miss Buhl sat naked on the ground, her mouth impossibly wide open. Beyond her only the scimitar edge of black rock and the echoing sky. He took a step forward. A rock fell, clattering, he swung round into a crouch. Bates, his face a rictus of hate and fear. Stone stepped back.

CRACK! A bullet smashed against the wall by his head. He ducked and began to run, back into the dark tunnel: blind again. He blundered off rough stone walls, hurting his hands using even the pain as a more useful guide as his dark-blinded eyes. Suddenly there was a vacancy beside him on his left: the other tunnel. He swerved and took it at a run. The walls crashed against him, tearing the shirt from his shoulders. The roof slapped him again. He rolled forward, clutching his damp head, wet now with blood. Onto his feet, plunging on. The screams were gaining volume once more, but they were not as loud as the footsteps and the grunting animalistic breathing close, too close, behind.

Suddenly the light slapped him in the face again. He

opened his eyes and slewed to a halt. He was on a ledge outside a cave in the cliff-face. It was a hundred feet down to the deep green sea and nowhere else to go. Stone swung round. Out of the darkness behind him passed a hard edge of shadow and into the blazing sunlight came a hand holding a gun. That was all. The gun was a big black Colt .45 automatic. The hand was red and black. There was skin hanging from it. Stone stepped back. Again. He gasped in a deep breath and leaped with all his force.

As Stone went over the edge the big Colt .45 spoke several times in rapid succession.

"Do you think we ought to have some sort of a service?" asked Mrs Gash suddenly.

"Mmmm?" asked Rebecca who had been day-dreaming.

"A service. I do. It's Sunday, you know. And I think we should thank the Lord we have been spared. Those of us who have. And ask that He look after the departed. And that He damn whoever is killing us all. Oh GOD." She shuddered until her teeth began to chatter.

They were keeping watch by Gant's watch-fire on the high plateau above the cliffs. Mrs Gash's eyes spilled tears. Her strength was returning, if not her strength of mind, and she wanted revenge. Not just for poor Letty Buhl but for all the confused mass of other victims. She shook her head fiercely. Her palm-frond hat fell off.

Rebecca Dark looked out to sea, her thoughts still miles away. It was early afternoon and the sun was agonisingly hot. Mrs Gash retrieved her hat. Rebecca pulled hers farther down on her tender forehead. She knew from bitter experience how much at risk the high bridge of her nose could be. They were all burned and peeling. They were lucky there had been no serious sunstroke. Rebecca looked at Mrs Gash. She was driving a short stick into the ground time after time after time. Her face was a sickly pink where the pallor of her flesh worked at odds with the livid red of her sunburn. Her eyes were ringed with crimson and seemed to have sunk into their sockets. There were new lines hard down either side of her nose and mouth. She looked so very old. She was muttering to herself. Rebecca had never seen a nervous breakdown but she guessed Mrs Gash was on the verge of one. She shifted uneasily, trying to work out whether it was actually Sunday. Immediately Mrs Gash was looking at her with button-bright eyes. "I think a service would be nice," wheedled the old lady.

"But who would hold one?"

"I could do it."

"Of course you could." Rebecca reassured her.

"And it is Sunday."

"Of course it is."

"So many dead."

"Yes."

"Who's doing it? Do you know who's doing it?" Mrs Gash asked.

"No of course I don't."

"I think it's that Mr Gant."

"No!"

"Or that Mr Stone."

"I don't think it's Mr Stone."

"Or Mr Wells."

"For Heaven's sake! Mr Wells is DEAD!"

"Well who then?"

"Oh, I don't know," Rebecca said, "I don't know. I don't know!" They sat for a while in angry silence. Then Mrs Gash said, "I think we should have a service."

"Well have one then."

155

"You can't have a service on your own."

"Then ask some of the others!" snapped Rebecca.

"Yes. I could do that. I'll ask that nice Mr Stone. He's always so kind and gentlemanlike. And Mr Gant, I like him."

"We'll ask everybody."

"That'll be nice, Letty. Can I preach a sermon?"

"If you like," said Rebecca, patiently.

"Or perhaps Mr Stone. I saw him at Stratford upon Avon in England, you know, he was acting in a play. I always think actors would make such good preachers. Except for their morals, of course. Like Burt Lancaster in that movie *Elmer Gantry*. Did you see that? I went to so many Meetings on the strength of that. But nothing ever came of it." She lapsed into silence.

Suddenly there was a distant sound immediately drowned by the screaming of disturbed birds.

"What was that?" asked Rebecca. Mrs Gash hadn't heard; didn't hear Rebecca asking. The birds settled down. Silence returned.

Almost immediately Gant came up, out of breath. "Have you seen Alec Stone?" he asked.

"Alec? No," said Rebecca, puzzled.

"He's gone."

Rebecca sat, utterly stunned by the news. Mrs Gash had risen and wandered to the cliff edge. "Oh look," she said. "There's somebody out for a swim."

"What!" yelled Gant. He dashed over beside her, with Rebecca close behind. Far below, there was a figure in the sea. They could just make out the fact that it was wearing a white shirt and black trousers. It was not swimming: it was sinking.

"Alec!" screamed Rebecca. "Alec!"

But Alec Stone had gone.

*   *   *

156

At breakfast next day the food gave out. Gant, who had spent all night watching over Rebecca, looked dully at the empty tin and drifted into a deep sleep. Mrs Gash wandered away to make sand castles.

Just after four, Rebecca woke up. She had collapsed upon seeing Stone's body in the water and had been unconscious for 24 hours. At this moment she was almost as helpless as Mrs Gash. She stared dully at the sky. There was no recognition in her eyes as they dwelt briefly on the sleeping figure of Eldridge Gant. She got up and went silently towards the makeshift latrine.

Stone's footprints led up towards the head of the waterfall. She did not recognize them, but she followed them to the pool by the small cliff. She waded into the pool because she felt dirty and she looked into the cave because she wondered where the water was coming from. She went inside because her curiosity was aroused and once inside, like a child, she had to explore farther.

Outside, Gant found her gone. He woke Slobowski and they began to look for her, calling out her name. Even in the tunnel Rebecca heard them and a strange terror washed over her. She had rejected Stone's death and the sound of their voices threatened to reawaken the pain. She froze like a frightened animal and then she ran away. She ran into the tunnel until the low roof stopped her then, in her blind panic, she gulped in a breath and dived underwater. Because the water deadened the painful voices she stayed under for as long as she could. The fear of drowning was a distant thing and she swam and swam.

When she stood up, the cave was like an abbey around her pulling the vague, august curves of its walls up above the random columns to the tiny point of light. She stood in the water until her teeth began to chatter and then she waded ashore. The pool was roughly saucer shaped and only a few feet deep at its deepest point by the tunnel so Rebecca had no difficulty in reaching the slippery shore. She stood on the chill rock bank and crossed her arms over her breast until her hands took her shoulders. She was still shivering. Her teeth were still chattering. She bit her tongue.

"Damn!" she said. DAMN DAMN DAMN Damn damn . . . amn...am... echoed the cave. She looked around in the uncertain light. It was enormous. She began to move through it. Like a whisper among the restless overwhelming tinkle of running water, came the sound of distant screaming. It grew louder. The cave was like some lower gallery in Hell. She sat down beside a stalagmite and closed her eyes, leaning back as though it were a tree.

The hand came out of nowhere and clamped around her mouth. She screamed but there was no sound. A finger bulged between her teeth and she bit down as hard as she could. There was a low, animal sound. She bit again. The hand tore away. She lurched into a half crouch and ran like a sprinter off her marks. There were footsteps behind her.

Then there was a passage in front of her. She ran into its utter darkness, cannoning off walls, bruising knees, thighs and shoulders but never falling. The screams washed over her. An acrid stench. She came round a tight curve and was bludgeoned to her knees by the light.

Her head filled with the screaming of birds, and something else. Her eyes searched the hard blue sky among the circling dots and brief flapping cruciforms of the gulls until . . .! A steady cross, black and far away.

A cross that roared instead of screaming, that flew level instead of soaring, that did not flap its wings. Suddenly it glinted in the sky like a jewel and the sky went out like a light.

Chapter Eight

The Outsiders

24 July–25 July

Guirat, NW India   *Night of 24 July*

"Don't move. Not a muscle," said Ram to Indira through clenched teeth, seeking to make the moment of their final ecstasy last as long as he could. Ram's back was supported by the angle of the wall. Indira's arms were wrapped tightly round his neck as his were tight round her waist, his hands on the cool, silken swells of her buttocks. He stood on both feet and she upon one, her right leg crooked around the top of his left thigh and hip. Only the strength of her arms and hip, and the rigid strength of his manhood, upon which she was ecstatically impaled, held her upright and they stood, entwined in the manner of the love-carvings of the great erotic friezes, in the corner of their bedroom. It was the night of their wedding day.

Ram had met Indira at Bombay University. A courtship had begun, followed the necessary forms, and ended today. Or was it yesterday? Ram would have looked at his watch but the movement might have ended the moment. They had travelled here to Guirat for the wedding because neither had any family and because Ram would begin his job as a Local Government official here in a few days. They were renting this room in a block of flats among

160

the southern suburbs of Rajkot, but, like all youngsters, dreamed of greater things.

Indira moved again, compliant with his wishes but unsure whether she approved of this esoteric form of love play. "Be still just a little longer," whispered Ram. His fingers traced the hollow of her spine up to the wings of her shoulder blades then back down to the full, slick swell of her magnificent buttocks.

It was nearly midnight. They had been making love languorously since sunset. They stood immobile for a little longer then Indira raised her face, almond eyes aglow, lips a little swollen with passion, and they began to kiss. The world shrank to the beating of their hearts, the heat of their bodies, the needs of their love. Ram felt Indira take control. Her belly rippled against his. Her tongue stabbed into his mouth. She closed upon him. He cried out, the sound trapped in the cave of their mouths.

The world lurched in the distance. The room shuddered. He threw out his hands, pressing back against the right-angled walls, to stop them falling. His head smashed back into the corner. Indira hurled against him, nails raking his back. Ram felt the rhythmic drive of his climax shake foundations in Karachi and Bombay, rip open the marshes in the Rann of Kutch, tumble the dizzy hills of Gir, tread like the left foot of Kali on Porbandar, Junagadh, Bavangar and Mahuva, hurling the very ocean over Bulsar and Surat. Three great convulsions then peace.

A little wind moved against their sated bodies, cooling, chilling. Ram opened his eyes and it was dark. Sometime during their climax the light had gone out. He looked up and saw the stars and the moon full and high. Ram looked down and saw the city of Rajkot in ruins at his feet. A distant explosion – a ball of fire first, then a sound. Screams came. Cries for help.

161

Indira sighed against his chest, noticing none of this. "Let's go to bed now," she whispered, "it's cold and I'm tired of standing." Her right leg eased down, standing beside his.

Ram looked wildly round, understanding but scarcely daring to believe. At the climax of their passion there had come a terrible earthquake to devastate Rajkot. It had destroyed their home, taken all the room except an angle of wall and this tiny corner that they stood in, 30ft above the ground. He explored with his toes. The floor ended a shrug way beyond Indira's heel.

The wall behind him was wet and cold. His back began to ache. Cramp came like a dagger in his groin. Indira moved against him, still far, far away. "Ram," she said.

"No," said Ram, through clenched teeth. "No, don't move! Not a muscle."

RAF Nimrod

"There!" yelled Nash.

"What? Where?" yelled Grokock.

Down there. An island I think. I'll go back and look from the window."

"Window!" muttered Flight Lieutenant Grokock under his breath, but the word was lost in the roar of the Nimrod's jets as he began to bring her round. Nash stumbled back down the fuselage until he got to a porthole on the side he wanted behind the broad wing. He shaded his eyes against the afternoon sun and looked again in the quicksilver glare of the sea.

There! Was it a shadow? He shook his head to clear his eyes, looked: and it was still there. "Yes!" he yelled into the microphone and the word sped to the pilot. "Right," answered the distant Grokock. "I see it. Going down." The plane tilted. Nash sat back.

Two days earlier he had introduced himself as a man called Andrews from Lloyds of London, and showed to Group Captain Sutton, Commanding Officer of the little RAF team training the Omani coastal command at Masirah an urgent request from several extremely high-ranking RAF officers that he do whatever Mr Andrews wanted. With Grokock and the crew, he had spent almost all of the succeeding 48 hours in the air, fruitlessly searching the area of *Wanderer*'s last known location.

Now, as the Nimrod moved across the sky towards the tiny comma of land, Nash pressed himself against the strengthened perspex of the port, searching for signs of life. At first there was nothing, then, at the rounded end of the island he saw a little light and a column of smoke began to drift towards India on the steady wind.

"It's them!" whispered Nash. "It must be them." He ran unsteadily up to the cockpit. Flight Lieutenant Grokock was on the radio. "What are you doing?" yelled Nash.

"Giving out their co-ordinates on the emergency wavelength. There should be some ships in the area. They'll get to them quicker than we can."

Nash stood very still. He should have thought of this. Christ, what a mess! The Americans and the Chinese both had ships close. The Russians, too, probably by now. And all of them would now know where the island was. "Was that wrong, sir?" Grokock was clearly confused.

"What? No, no. Of course not. Standard practice. But I was just thinking. . . . Look, they might be in immediate trouble down there. We'll drop them the emergency supplies, and I'll jump myself. Go down and lend a hand. Do you need to de-pressurise?"

163

"I'm afraid I can't allow that, sir."

Nash didn't have time to argue. He showed him his real SIS ID card. There was a spare parachute with the supplies. Nash went back down the length of the aircraft and strapped it on. "Which is the radio?" he bellowed over the rush of air as the co-pilot opened the door.

"This one, sir."

"Thanks. Better keep my eye on it. Dump it last." He helped throw the boxes of supplies out as the aircraft roared low over the length of the island, and then jumped himself.

He landed, shaken but unhurt, on a beach beside the radio and close to quite a sizeable rock. He looked around: nobody about. He picked up the radio, carried it to the rock and dropped it. There was a muffled crash. He walked away and began to pack up his parachute. A tall man appeared over a rise, paused, then came forward, hand outstretched but eyes wary.

"Eldridge Gant," he said. "And we are sure glad to see you!"

"Perry Andrews from Lloyds," said Nash, grasping Gant's hand. "Came to see if you were all right and to wet-nurse the radio."

"Radio!" said Gant. "Boy can we use one of them!" He went over to the radio's box and squatted down. "We need all the help we can get!" He threw the words over his shoulder. "We seem to have some kind of lunatic amongst us. He's murdered most of the survivors. But with this we can . . ." His voice trailed off and he turned towards Nash, his face dead. "It's broken," he said.

"Oh damn," said Nash automatically. "Now I wonder how the hell that happened?"

164

Hannegan the helicopter pilot burst into Lydecker's cabin without knocking. "It's in, Ed. We just picked it up on the radio."

"What's in?"

"Location of the survivors from *Wanderer*."

"The hell you say! Over the radio?"

"Some Limey flyboy on Emergency."

"How far?"

"Six hours."

They had been searching for over a week: now they would be there by midnight. Midnight! He remembered what an old friend, an old Spook had once said to him. "Don't trust the dark. She's a whore. She'll make you the Invisible Man so you think you can't be beaten, but at the same time she's turning all the Opposition into Invisible Men as well. I've seen more guys killed by the dark . . ." Lydecker jerked himself off his bunk and went to see the Captain.

The island resolved itself into a firm shape off the port beam at 2343. *Lincoln* had been running without lights since before 2300, just in case. They went in slowly and anchored to the south, just off-shore to windward of the massive cliffs, and Lydecker led in his tiny force with their bulky black equipment in fat, black, little rubber boats onto the sand of a small bay. They disembarked quietly onto the deserted beach and moved forward.

On the beach was the charred skeleton of a boat. At the top of the rise above the beach an unmarked grave. By a pool among some palm trees an old fire, supplies and parachutes. "There's only one with harness for a man," Hannegan told Lydecker, his whisper covered by the sound of a waterfall. There was nobody around. They set up their equipment as an ambush and began to move up the island.

The ground gathered itself up into a steep slope covered with rough grass. Then this levelled off into a deserted plateau where a black circle still held a little of a fire's warmth. They began to move back down the island but stopped for a discussion on the slope. "Where in hell are they?" asked Lydecker.

"Christ knows," said Hannegan. They stood, uncertain of what to do next. There was a little silence. Then . . .

"What's that?" whispered Lydecker urgently.

"Shooting," answered one of the others out of the darkness.

"Yeah, but where is it coming from?" They all listened intently. Then Hannegan suddenly knelt and put his ear to the ground.

"Down there," he said.

The Russian submarine

Beria swung into the cupboard which the Captain laughingly referred to as their stateroom, and called to the sleeping Andropov with a voice as excited as his face. "They're on an island. Someone has just broadcast an emergency call giving its position."

"How far?"

"About eight hours if we go on the surface."

They spent time discussing whether or not it might be a trap. The Captain was of this opinion, for his charts showed no island at the stated location. But a week of inactivity had galled the two KGB men and, trap or not, they were going to look. If there was anything there then they would venture further on their own.

166

The lookout saw the island just after 0110 local time on the morning of 25 July. The submarine approached the island from the north-east. Beria and Andropov loaded a few token medical supplies into a rubber dinghy and, trying to look like genuine rescuers, they set off a little after 0130. The submarine turned away behind them, retiring to safer waters. It would return each hour to this rendezvous.

It took the Federal Security men more than 15 minutes to reach the island. They beached the dinghy on a low sand spit, which was the curling tail of the land, and climbed silently ashore. Then they spent the next half hour searching fruitlessly for any survivors. While they were standing on the cliffs, looking north in the bright moonlight, Beria saw the ship. "Down!" he snapped. It was coming in from the north-west slowly and without lights. They watched it stop and put down a boat. It was 0220.

"Come on," whispered Beria, "we'll go down the other side." They went across the cliffs quickly and began to run back down the slope. This time it was Andropov because he was in the lead.

"Yuri! There's another one!" *Lincoln* lay also without lights, to the south of the island. A boat was pulling away, full of men. "It was a trap!" yelled Andropov, panicking. After all, he was not a field agent. And he suddenly saw the horrifying possibility that he might even be responsible for the first really embarrassing international incident involving the Federal Security Service.

"I don't think so," said Beria more calmly. "Let's go!"

They ran towards their dinghy; it was 0226. They paused for breath in some scrub by a small pool at the head of a waterfall.

"What do we do now?" asked Andropov, frankly by now out of his depth. Beria rubbed the back of his hand over his

167

mouth and chin. "We wait, I think. We're too late for the rendezvous anyway."

They sat in silence, gasping, Suddenly in the sigh of the wind from the north-east came a muffled detonation, followed by a strange metallic sound.

"What's that?" muttered Andropov.

"Grapnels," said Beria. "Someone's coming up the cliffs." The wind backed abruptly, carrying voices from the south-west, with the crunch of a landing boat. "The other boat," whispered Andropov.

Then, in the water right beside them, a loud bubbling splash. They shrank back into the bushes. Out of the pool under the cliff waded someone carrying in one hand a torch, and in the other a huge black Colt .45 automatic pistol.

Glorious Revolution

The Bee leaned against the guard rail at the very point of the bows like some strange figurehead on the *Glorious Revolution*. His eyes probed the darkness as though he could see the island upon which he was certain he would find his beloved Hummingbird although he knew very well it was eight hours' sailing time away. He was in his mind already on the little piece of land, discovering and rescuing his lover, alone, like a hero of romance.

The sea boiled around the bow throwing up glinting salt spray. The moon was low, fat and full – a pitiless cover from the darkness.

The Bee had always loved the dark because it hid things. As a child in Shanghai whenever he wished to hide he found the darkest corner and crawled into it until he became part of it. He had hidden much as a child, for his father had been a Western sailor who had loved his mother and left her. From the earliest moments of his life he had had pale skin, big ears, a long bony face and round eyes. All this he had been forced to wear like a terrible scar for the children in his neighbourhood laughed at him, fought him, drove him into the dark corners. But there came a day when he had begun to fight back.

He fought physically at first, but then intellectually also and as he beat them on the street with his fists, he beat them in the classroom with hard work. He became a star pupil. But they still laughed behind their sleeves. He worked even harder and won a scholarship to Beijing University.

The night before he left he raped the sister of his greatest enemy. The experience had disappointed him. In Beijing also he had been an outcast and in consequence a star pupil. His speciality was languages. He impressed his tutors. He impressed a man whose offices were in 15 Bowstring Alley. The chances of his parentage, birth and upbringing made him a perfect agent: he was secretive, lonely, hardworking, meticulous; he hated himself as well as everybody else and in consequence found it no strain to assume other characters for great lengths of time; he had come to terms with this self-hate, however, because he had proved himself superior to the people who had begun it – therefore, although he remained utterly ruthless, there was little chance of him becoming utterly psychopathic and breaking down, in the short term at least.

He met the Hummingbird on his last course before becoming fully operative as a SAD agent. All he could think was how beautiful this person seemed to him. It always seemed strange to the Bee that the beautiful Hummingbird returned his feelings. They became a team. The Bee was the thinker, the planner, the Control; the Hummingbird was the executive. Singly they were dangerous, together they became deadly.

At 0220 local time the Bee was rowing silently towards the island in the small black rubber dinghy, his heart thunderous in his broad chest at the prospect of seeing his beautiful Hummingbird again. He had a powerful gun designed to launch a grapnel up cliffs in excess of 200 ft in height. At the foot of the north-eastern cliffs he knelt in the unsteady dinghy and fired this upwards. It arched against the moonbright sky and over the edge of the cliff.

He pulled it. It held. He had a torch, a pistol, and a light machine-gun. He secured them all to his body and began to climb. By 0235 he was on the edge of the cliff. He moved forward swiftly and silently. There was a sound of falling water: he went towards it. Then, a little way in front, he heard a scuffle of movement. He stopped. The sound came again. His heart was like an earthquake in his chest. He whistled their call sign. It was returned. He called, "Hummingbird."

An indistinct shape moved in the dark, splashing in water. He raised his torch. "*Don't!*" cried the Hummingbird. Too late. The Bee saw the Hummingbird there in the pool of light. He began to scream.

Indian Ocean

Just after they had all gone back to the island for the second time, the Radio Operator on the *Lincoln* picked up the first emergency broadcast. He went to the bridge at a run. "What is it?" asked the Captain. The Radio Operator told him.

"Mary, Mother of God!" The Captain swung round. "Slip the anchor. Full steam ahead. Give me searoom!"

The Radio Operator mentioned the men on the island.

"They stand a damn sight more chance than we do. Engine Room? Give me flank speed NOW! Somebody get

170

Hannegan the 'chopper pilot up here!" *Lincoln* began to move: it was 0240.

The Radio Operator on *Glorious Revolution* finished relaying the Bee's final message to Beijing. He turned the dial and caught the end of the message. He listened. It was repeated. He ran to the Officer of the watch who ran to the bridge and told the Captain. The Captain went dead white and ordered full speed. The ship began to move: it was 0255.

The submarine Commander looked at his watch. "They are late. We will return in an hour." The submarine turned on the surface and began to move out to sea. The Radio Operator was not at his post because absolute radio silence was being observed. The Emergency message was never received. The alarm was raised by one of the watch. "What's that?" the man suddenly demanded. Everyone on the submarine's high fin jumped.

"What?" snarled the Commander.

"I'm not sure, sir. There." He gestured towards the north-east. The Commander took a pair of night glasses and peered into the dark. At first he saw nothing, then . . . an unsteady white mass . . . glinting . . . coming . . . The Commander smashed his fist onto the communications button. "Dive-dive-dive!" he screamed. "Crash dive. Now!" The submarine tilted. The water began to break over her. It was 0300.

171

Chapter Nine

Kali

24 July–25 July

"Quiet!" yelled Eldridge Gant. "Will you be QUIET!"

"Can you hear something?" asked Mrs Gash. "Is it Rebecca?"

"No."

"Is it Letty?"

"THERE!" He pointed up among the circling birds. It was an aeroplane. It caught the light like a jewel in the sky. "The fire," he yelled. "Quick! The fire!" They ran the last few hundred yards up the island to the pile of sticks on the height of the cliffs. Gant was fumbling in his pocket for matches, swearing under his breath with the strain of the excitement. He fell on his knees by the fire, matches out, hands shaking too much. He spilt some, grabbed one, lit it. It went out. Slobowski and Mrs Gash arrived and clustered round. He lit another. "Is it still there?"

"Yup." From the phlegmatic Chicagoan.

"Hurry!" twittered Mrs Gash. The single match was useless. He fumbled out three more and lit them all at once, pushing them into the kindling. "Burn," he whispered. "Burn for Christsake!"

Flames seared his fingertips, small but blossoming. The wind stirred. "It's coming," observed Slobowski. Gant took the last of the matches to the other side of the fire and the flames once again were small. He blew, terrified that his shaky breath would extinguish them altogether. They grew, took root in the wood. Smoke billowed into Gant's face. He choked, eyes streaming. "Come on round . . . that's it," said Slobowski to the aeroplane. Mrs Gash began to cry. It came closer, lower. The roar of its jet engines grew, steady, reliable. It was coming in. "Here!' Here!" they cried, but it already knew.

It came over low, from the sea, scattering the raucous birds and thundering towards the low spit, causing the earth to quake under their feet. Its side was open. Things began to fall out. Boxes, packages blossoming parachutes as they fell. Finally, in the distance, a man, falling towards the far point of the island. The plane pulled up, turned, came back past them. The wings wagged: it was like a slow wink from an old friend. Slobowski waved. Mrs Gash yoo-hoo'd through her tears.

Gant was already running down the island to where the man would come to earth. Head up, shoulders back, legs long, he ran as fast as he could over the scrub grass down the slope, past the sounding waterfall, through the clearing, over the dunes and there he was.

"Hey! Hi! Hello!" He strode over the final ridge and down onto the beach, hand outstretched. He saw a man above medium height clad in light khaki shirt and slacks. He had the bearing of a military man. Greying hair. Clipped moustache. Level grey-blue eyes.

"Eldridge Gant," said Gant as their hands joined in a firm handshake. "And we are sure glad to see you!"

"Perry Andrews from Lloyds'" said the man. He had an English accent as clipped as his moustache. "Came down to see if you are all OK and to wet-nurse the radio."

"Radio! Boy can we use one of them." Gant went to it.

173

It was in a heavy leather protective case, strapped shut. He squatted down and began to undo the straps. Now he could really be of some use – get the bastard who had been doing all the murders . . . Call the Marines . . . He was dizzy with simple relief. "We need all the help we can get," he said over his shoulder. His fingers were busy. First strap back. "We seem to have some kind of lunatic loose amongst us." Second strap back. "But with this we can . . ." Open the lid; broken glass. Smashed dials. He looked at the Englishman Andrews. "It's broken."

"Oh damn! Now I wonder how the hell that could have happened?" He came over and squatted down. He smelt of aftershave, soap and talcum powder. Plausible son of a bitch, thought Gant. "I say, I'm most terribly sorry," the man continued. "Still, help's on the way." It hasn't sunk in, thought Gant, about Spooner, Laughton, Wells, Stone, the others. "It will be too late," he said wearily. "He'll just be trying all the harder now."

"Who?"

"Whoever this bastard is who's trying to kill us all. Slobowski! It has to be Slobowski. But I just cannot prove a thing."

"What . . ."

Slobowski and Mrs Gash arrived. "This is Mr Andrews," said Gant.

"Perry Andrews. How do you do? From Lloyds of London. Insurance investigator. The tall man was up, offering to shake hands, still utterly unaware of the atmosphere. "Thought I might be of some service. Where are the others? Have you any wounded?"

"We haven't anyone, period," said Slobowski.

"What!" Now the newcomer was shocked. "Just three of you?"

174

"Four," said Slobowski. "If Miss Dark is still around here somewhere."

Rebecca! thought Gant. "My God. Rebecca. We must find Rebecca." He too was on his feet.

"She's quite vanished, you know," said Mrs Gash. "Not a sign, . . . Gant flung himself past her, fighting to get his gun out. "What have you done with her, you . . ."

"Naaaw!" yelled Slobowski. He smashed one huge fist into Gant's shoulder sending him crashing to the ground. He swung his boot back, mad with rage. "That's quite enough," snapped the stranger. Suddenly he had a gun.

Nash's mind was reeling in confusion. Three, maybe four, out of how many aboard *Wanderer*? And where was Alec Stone? Perhaps, he hoped, aware that it was a very faint hope, perhaps there were more boats, another island. But what was going on here? What on earth could have happened to reduce these people to this? And in just over a week. "Perhaps it would be a good idea if somebody explained to me. Mr Gant, would you mind?"

"I told you," said Gant. "This murdering . . ."

"From the beginning, if you don't mind."

"There's no time. You don't understand."

"Now!" Nash's voice was like a whiplash.

"OK," said Gant wearily. He picked himself up. "There were twelve of us. Miss Dark, Mrs Gash, you Slobowski, Miss Buhl, Mr Spooner, Wells, Stone, O'Keefe, Bates, Laughton, Slattery and myself."

"Twelve where?" asked Nash.

"In the lifeboat. The only lifeboat."

"But the rest of the crew, the Captain . . .?" Slobowski shook his head. Gant shrugged. Nash was utterly stunned. "All?" he whispered. "All except twelve?"

"You ain't heard nothing yet," said Slobowski.

It was almost dark now. "I'll light a fire, shall I?" said

Mrs Gash drifting off towards the camp. Nash put his gun away.

"Rebecca," said Gant.

"Ain't nothing we can do," Slobowski consoled him, but all he received was a look of virulent hatred in reply.

Mrs Gash, good as her word, was cooking some of the emergency supplies when they got to the camp.

"Go on," said Nash.

"Spooner went first. He fell overboard on the lifeboat. O'Keefe went the same way. We think they must have been murdered somehow. Someone salted our water, nearly did for all of us but we saw the island. We've been here since the 19th. Slattery went first. Throat cut. Then Laughton and Wells were blown up in the boat. It was booby-trapped. Then Miss Buhl. She just vanished. We only ever found her clothes. Then Bates, he went over the edge of the cliff looking for birds' eggs to eat. Then Stone yesterday. Just vanished. Then we saw him floating at the bottom of the cliffs. And Rebecca today. She just vanished too. We were looking for her when you arrived."

Nash looked at them with horror. Three lean, burned, unkempt animals, matter-of-factly telling him of this incredible mayhem. He didn't know what to believe. Logic demanded that it had to be one of them, if they were telling the truth. Or two, or all. His head spun. They watched him, eyes bright in the firelight. Mad. Nine people. Alec Stone. Perhaps they had eaten them. He had read in the papers about something like that. But nine people! And Alec Stone.

None of them ate the basic rations that Mrs Gash prepared, but she had found some coffee and they gulped it down with the added luxury of a little powdered milk. Then Eldridge Gant got up. "Look," he said, "I've got to

176

look for Rebecca. I have to. I can't just sit here. I can't!"
The strong voice was dangerously near to cracking, as was
the man. They all rose to their feet. "I think we'd better all
stick together," said Nash.

"Are there any torches?" asked Slobowski.

"I don't know," said Nash. They looked. They found
three that worked.

They started at the point of the island and worked their
way up towards the cliffs. They started a little after 0900.
By 1100 they were on the main hump of the slope above
the waterfall. They were strung in a thin line within calling
distance of each other. The birds were asleep. The sea and
wind were quiet. Mrs Gash, in the middle of the line,
heard it first.

"What's that?" she called. Gant ran towards her.

"There!" she cried. "Again! It's Rebecca." They all arrived
and stood gasping. A distant cry came, faint and strangely
echoing.

"It is Rebecca!" said Gant, wildly. "Where is it coming from?"

"Down there?" Nash, hardly believing it, pointing his
torch to the ground. Mrs Gash took a few eager steps
forward, screamed and half vanished into a hidden hole.
She started to slip almost immediately but Gant caught her
wrists and pulled her out. Rebecca's screams were suddenly
louder.

"Rebecca!" screamed Gant. "Can you hear?"

"Yes-es-es," echoed Rebecca's voice. "Help! Oh help!"

"Where are you?"

"Cave-ave-ave." Faint, but quite clear.

"Did you fall in? Rebecca did you fall?"

"No. Waterfall . . . fall . . . all . . ."

"What?" yelled Gant.

"Pool above the wat . . ." Silence. They screamed her

name but there was no reply. So they ran as fast as they could down to the pool above the waterfall.

By torchlight, the cave behind the pool above the waterfall was quite small. The roof of the tunnel came down abruptly almost to the surface of the water giving it a claustrophobic air when lit, which it lacked in the dark. Gant waded forward to the tunnel entrance, flashlight and gun at the ready.

Nash said, "Just a moment," and Gant paused. "You've got spare bullets? In case you need to reload quickly?" Gant nodded and patted his waterproof belt. As he did so, Slobowski ducked into the tunnel and Mrs Gash followed immediately before anyone could stop her. Gant followed. Nash brought up the rear.

Slobowski came up suddenly into the main cave. He stood up breathing quietly. The tunnel had been surprisingly short. The water erupted beside him: Mrs Gash heaved herself upright. Gant and Nash arrived almost simultaneously, both well armed.

"Do all Lloyds' men carry guns, Mr Andrews?" whispered Gant. Nash's teeth glinted in the gloom. He made no reply.

Then several things happened at once: Mrs Gash sneezed loudly; a bright, dazzling torch-beam cut across the cave catching Slobowski frozen with surprise; there was a flat report and a spurt of flame by the torch; and Slobowski gave an explosive grunt, spinning off his feet to slap into the water. Even before the spray fell, two more shots kicked up the water beside his body. The others were heading for shore and cover as fast as they could.

The light moved restlessly, searching for them. It found Mrs Gash. Again the flat report, echoing; as though a giant had clapped his hands. Gant caught Mrs Gash as she stumbled and at last thought to squeeze off a shot of his own in reply. It cracked angrily off a rock. The beam wavered.

178

Nash also shot at the torch. He was helping the wounded Slobowski to the other side of the pool and it was only a quick, inaccurate shot but the torch nevertheless went out. Darkness closed in, and, beneath the maddening fell-like tintinnabulation of the running water, silence.

"You all right?" whispered Nash to Slobowski.

"Arm," he whispered back. "Think it's broke."

"Bleeding?"

"Don't know."

"ANDREWS?" Gant's voice, echoing from everywhere.

"Yes?" answered Nash, his voice echoing also, giving away no target."

"How's Slobowski?"

"Fine. Mrs Gash?"

"Fine," answered Gant's disembodied voice. Nash smiled. With any luck this free and cheerful communication would be doing the enemy's morale no good at all. But then Gant's voice came again, its timbre slightly changed, its intonation, as though the actor had become slightly drunk.

"Andrews?" It called. Nash thought, Don't make too much of a good thing – but he answered, "Yes?"

"I'm going to kill you."

What? Nash's hair rose. His flesh prickled.

"Kill you . . . you . . . oo . . . oooo." And it wasn't Gant at all. Christ! Talk about turning the tables. He rubbed a shaking hand down a sweat-slicked face. Their adversary had suddenly gained the superhuman power of lunacy in his mind. It was as though he were trapped in the middle of Hitchcock's *Psycho* or Carpenter's *Halloween*.

The mad are always so much more powerful than the sane.

CRACK! A shot away to the right. Gant answered, his gun giving away his position.

179

"Gant!" yelled Nash. "Don't fire back like that. He can move quicker than you can with Mrs Gash."

"Clever, clever, Mr Andrews." The voice was no longer an imitation of Gant's. It was high, singsong, utterly insane. Nash's hair stirred again. "Let's see you get out of this one then." The light stabbed on. Nash's arms snapped up immediately without thought, ready to destroy this thing as he would a spider, centipede or scorpion.

"No!" Gant's voice cut through his revulsion. Gant's torch stabbed on momentarily, revealing something. A shot from the murderer sent dust smoking into its beam and then it was gone. Nash stared with glare-blinded eyes at the after image of what Gant's torch had revealed.

A tall black column of rock, running with water and glistening like a slug's back. Against it, a girl, arms up, tied at wrist, waist and ankle as a shield. She was gagged. Was she really naked?

They were in a triangle, the gunman, Gant and Nash. They'd never get behind him: he could use a torch but they could not. Nash lifted his head. Brightness and a shot. He ducked back amid a shower of rock fragments. Christ! That was close. Stalemate, thought Nash.

Mexican standoff, thought Gant. He raised his head. The beam of the murderer's torch was worrying the far side of the cave. Was Andrews all right? Mrs Gash stirred and groaned. The light swung back to them. Gant ducked automatically. There was no shot. Silence and the running of water down the cover walls. What now?

"Gant!" It was the high, mad voice of the human, totally unlike any voice Gant knew. "Gant, I'm tired of playing this game. Stand up now." Stand up? Christ! "STAND UP OR I SHOOT THE GIRL." The girl . . . Gant looked up. Light on Rebecca. The gun low on her belly. Very low and digging in. Her head shaking wildly. "If I pull the

180

trigger now it'll blow her guts out. She'll still be alive GANT!"

"All right! ALL RIGHT!"

"And the others."

Gant began to get up. Andrews away on the right, climbing to his feet, beaten.

"Throw the guns in the water." Splash. Splash.

"Step forward. Hands high." Gant moved forward, slowly. The light licked at him then swung away towards Andrews. There was a shot. Andrews staggered back and began to topple. The light flashed back onto Gant. He closed his eyes and stopped. No Broadway. No London. No *Long Day's Journey into Night* that he regretted most of all. He stood still and took a deep breath. CRACK! CRACK!

Two shots. Darkness. He threw himself to the ground, rolling. He stopped and lay on his back, opening his eyes slowly. There was no pain. He moved. It washed over him – a great joy: he was alive and unharmed. How could this be?

CRACK! A cone of flame dead ahead. Behind the gunman?

BEHIND THE GUMMAN!

There were footsteps. A confused scuffle. Where was his torch? A scream. Hoarse and masculine from the shadows ahead. Andrews' torch blazed, wavered, searched. Found two vague shapes wrestling in the shadows. Gant made for Rebecca at a dead run. He fumbled across the dark cave stumbling and hitting his shins. The two men wrestled away to the right. Andrews' torch didn't show much. He made it to Rebecca. She was tied with rope. Gagged with her own shirt. The knots were slippery and wet. He took the gag out first. "Are you all right?"

". . .es. . ." He wrestled with the well-tied and recalcitrant knots, tearing his fingernails. But they were loosening. Her hands came free at last. She groaned as she lowered her stiff arms. The knot at her waist was easier. Then her ankles and she was free. He supported her back down the cave. Andrews' torch beam began to slide away. Then it wavered for a moment, and fell. Darkness. A clatter from where the men wrestled. The abrupt slap of a blow. One of them fell. A rattle of stones. Running footsteps – running away. Silence.

Then the gunman's torch blazed on. Gant threw Rebecca behind a rock and dived after her. There was no shot: only slow, purposeful footsteps. The light fastened on this rock, making a halo round its edge, intensifying as the torch drew near like sunrise behind a mountain. Then suddenly it was on them. Gant threw a protective arm across Rebecca like the hero of a melodrama. He felt silly: it was all he could think of to do as he looked into the heart of the light.

"Are you O.K.?" asked Alec Stone from behind the brightness of the torch.

It was too much for Rebecca. She began to scream. Gant shook her but it did no good. His own mind was reeling: Stone. Stone back from the dead. "How?" he began.

"No time now," Stone took Rebecca's rigid form and folded it over his broad shoulder in a fireman's lift. Then he was off towards Mrs Gash, the gunman's torch carefully lighting his way. Mrs Gash had been shot in the leg. There was a small wound in her thigh welling blood sluggishly: almost like tar in the torchlight. "You'd better help her," said Stone. Gant tried to wake her up.

"Who else?" asked Stone.

"Slobowski and the Englishman. Over there."

"Englishman?"

"Andrews. From Lloyd's. So he says." Still with Rebecca over his shoulder, Stone waded over to the far side of the lake. Slobowski lay behind a large rock. He had been shot high on the right side of his chest. Nasty but not too serious.

The Englishman lay a little farther on. Another chest wound. This one was serious. Stone went unsteadily down on one knee. "How does it feel, Soldier?"

"Pretty bad, Alec." He coughed red foam. "Christ! Hurts!"

Stone nodded. "Hang on."

"I'm not going anywhere." Nash watched Stone put down the inert body of the girl. Reality came and went. He would hardly have recognized Stone. The massive quiet competence which now invested the man. The change was amazing. It held all of Soldier Nash's attention while his quiet executive took off his ragged white shirt and wadded it up as a rudimentary pressure-bandage. "Thanks, old son."

"You'll be all right. You know what they say. . . ."

"Yes. Old soldiers never die. . . ."

"Gant."

"Yes?"

"Slobowski and Nash are pretty bad. Is there any First Aid stuff?"

"The aircraft dropped some. I'll go." He propped Mrs Gash against a boulder, and, wondering who Nash was – who Stone was, for that matter – he waded into the lake. He ducked under the blackrock lintel, took a few steps through the tunnel, erupted out of the cave and took the slope down to the camp at a dead run. Here he began to heave the boxes around looking for the First Aid kit.

Suddenly there were lights. Blinding, transfixing. Like stage lights. He rocked back on his heels, shading his eyes with his hands. He could see only brightness. All right buster, gettem up."

"Get what up where?" He wasn't being funny. He wasn't being smart. He wasn't even being brave: he was simply too stunned to react.

"All right Hannegan," said someone else. The second

man moved into the brightness. He was dressed in black. His face was blacked. Gant was jerked back to his early Special Forces days.

"Ed Lydecker," said the man in black. Gant got up. He was a little taller than Lydecker. "Eldridge Gant," he said. There was a pause, then Lydecker shoved out his hand. "I wouldn't have recognized you, sir."

Gant shook the hand. "Look," he said. "I don't know who you people are, but we have some wounded men up in the cave back there."

"I see. Hannegan, take some men and medication. And go in quietly."

"Very quietly," said Gant, and told them how to get in. After they left, he collapsed quietly onto the sand. Lydecker looked down at him. God, he looked old: old and beat. "What's been going on here, sir?"

Silence.

"Mr Gant, sir?" Gant's head rolled back on his thin neck. His eyes were still half closed. "Where're you from, Mr Lydecker?"

"Off the ship out there." He gestured towards *Lincoln*.

"How did you find us?"

"Radio message from a 'plane, sir."

"Why all this?"

"Precautions, sir. We heard shooting." He shrugged. Gant shook his head slowly. Well, thought Lydecker, if I'd been marooned for a week and more maybe I'd be a mite strange myself. "How many are there of you altogether, sir?" he asked gently. Gant flinched as though he had been struck. "Six I think," he said.

"Six off the *Wanderer*?" Lydecker was stunned. "What about the other survivors?"

"Five off *Wanderer*. One Englishman who parachuted

184

in with the supplies. There are no more." Lydecker simply didn't believe it.

There was a scrape of footsteps, voices. Lydecker's gun came up. "All right, Ed. Only us." It was Hannegan back. They had a man with a grey mustache on an improvised stretcher, and were supporting a second whose chest and shoulder were bound. There was a broad, powerful looking man who had no shirt helping a girl dressed in Hannegan's black blouse supporting an older woman.

"Is that *all*?" he asked Hannegan.

"No," said the man without the shirt in an English accent, "There's one more. We'll have to go back for him in a while." There was some deep meaning hidden in these words. Gant stirred: "You want to go back in now, Alec?"

"Sorry, sir," said Lydecker. "I'm not letting any of you out of my sight until we've got some of this cleared up. We'll take you back to the ship now, if you don't mind." Gant began to disagree but the Englishman stopped him: "It's all right. He's not going anywhere. We'll be back."

"I could send in a couple of men to look for him," offered Lydecker. "Is he hurt too?"

"God, I hope so," said the Englishman, then he stopped and seemed to collect himself. "No. You wouldn't find him and your men would stand no chance at all. I'll come back."

"And I'll come back," said Gant. There was something in their voices which made Lydecker shiver.

They went down to the beach and wearily climbed into the dinghies. They left the lights in place, but switched them off. They needed the space for the stretcher and the wounded. For those who could climb, there was a ladder down *Lincoln's* side. For those who could not, a stretcher came down from the gantries.

As he climbed onto the deck, Lydecker checked his watch: it was after one. He went down with the survivors to the sickbay. They were wrapped in blankets and given coffee to drink. They were pale, hollow-eyed, thin. The men had fairly heavy beards. They all stank. They had the look of an outing from a lunatic asylum. Ludecker was put in mind of *One Flew Over the Cuckoo's Nest.* On the island, in the wind, they looked dangerous. Here under electric lights, surrounded by normality, they looked helpless, mindless: dead beat.

Stone and Gant were restless. As soon as the Ship's doctor had examined them they began to prowl around the sickbay like animals in a cage. Eventually Gant turned to Lydecker. "We want to go back now," he said.

"Back?"

"To the island. We have unfinished business."

Stone said, "There's a man back there who killed six innocent people. I want him."

"What?" Lydecker could hardly believe the enormity of the crime. "Are you *sure*?" How could he tell Abe Parmilee? He took them through to his own cabin. "Right," he said. "You said six."

Gant told them off on his fingers: "Slattery, Spooner, Wells, Bates, Laughton, Miss Buhl."

"Close," said Stone, "but not quite correct: Spooner, O'Keefe, Slattery, Laughton, Miss Buhl, Bates. It was Wells all along."

"Wells? WELLS! But I saw him *burn*."

There was a silence. Gant sat down. "Explain to me," he said.

"Spooner was first," said Stone. "He was at the tiller when it broke during the storm. You remember?" Gant nodded. "Good. The tiller broke. He asked for an oar. We passed one down. You and Rebecca had one end.

Then Slobowski, Laughton and myself. Then O'Keefe, Wells, Bates, Mrs Gash, Miss Buhl and Slattery. Wells, you notice, was in the middle, between O'Keefe and Bates. Now what occurred to me was this. If you want to control a lever, then you go to the fulcrum, as though you are balancing a see-saw.

"In that situation, you, Gant, for instance, would have had to have exerted enormous force in order to jerk the far end of the oar over into Spooner. At the other end it might have been easier, but not much more so. In the middle, however, it is a very much easier task. Consider: he would have had a firm anchor in those of us behind him in the bows. Between him and Spooner, there was Bates, then the two women, then Slattery who had very little purchase on the paddle-end of the oar. He would have had the earliest job of all, you see." They digested this in silence. Then Lydecker said, "But it could have been O'Keefe or Bates."

"Yes," said Stone.

"Why didn't you say anything?" asked Gant.

"I didn't work it out until we made the island."

"And is this all you have to base your accusation on?"

"No. There's more."

"Evidence," demanded Gant.

"No evidence. I can't even tell you for certain. I've fought with him hand to hand and I still couldn't swear to his identity. But I think I've worked out the murders in the boat."

"O'Keefe?" asked Gant.

"That's a bit more complex. It was our watch. First he suggested the lamp. That was important. I agreed. We lit it. Then he asked for a cigarette although he didn't smoke. He dropped the case. Foolishly I bent to pick it up. He swung the tiller, the boom came across, hit me, knocked me out. That's fact. Now for some surmise. While I was

187

out he salted the water. O'Keefe was only pretending to be asleep. He saw Wells and gave himself away somehow. Wells killed him, sat him up straight, put the Very pistol in his lap. Then he floated the lamp in the water, waited until it had drifted some way away, then woke me up. I noticed the lamp was gone – he said it had fallen overboard. He woke Slattery and oversaw my medicinal whisky.

"By good luck Slattery saw the light. It looked pretty good heaving around out there. It was a small light close by, but we lacked anything to judge its size by and it could have been a ship's light far away. So we all went wild, except O'Keefe. Wells took the pistol from him and talked to him. We all watched the flares. Then someone staggered, the boat rocked, the boom swung and knocked O'Keefe overboard. We were still watching the flares, looking for the light."

"And you think O'Keefe was dead then?" asked Gant. "But I saw him move."

"He was face-down in the water. He was quite still. Then the sharks came in. He didn't move until the sharks hit him. And he didn't cry out."

"The boom could have knocked him out."

"Yes. But he was face-down in the water. If he had been breathing he would have choked. And he stayed quiet when the sharks hit. I don't know. Maybe he was so far out he genuinely didn't notice, but I really and truly think that a live man being torn to pieces by sharks is going to mention it to someone."

"Yes," said Lydecker. "I'm inclined to agree. Anyone else?"

"No. On the island it got too open. He stopped leaving traces."

"But he *died*," said Gant. "I saw him *BURN*."

"Yes. There might be something there, too."

188

"What is there in a walking bonfire?"

"Look at it like this. Apart from Spooner, taken by chance, all the other murders were secret, almost personal. But this was public, spectacular. Why? Because he wanted to convince us. Think how much easier it would be for him with us thinking he was dead. He had certainly found the cave by then and now all he wanted was to move into it. He could have just disappeared, of course, but then we might have suspected too soon."

"Wait," said Gant. "If it took us so long to find the cave, how come he did it so quickly?"

"What were you looking for on the island?"

"I don't know . . . something to eat . . . a way to get off . . . a way to stay alive."

"And all he was looking for was a place to hide. While you were looking at the sea, the cliffs, the outside, he was looking at holes, caves, tunnels . . ."

"Yeah. I see. But I still don't see how he burned."

"There was a way. Remember we found Wells drinking out of a hip flask after the water had been salted on the lifeboat?"

"Yes, whisky."

"Ever see that flask again?"

"No."

"What are you getting at, Mr Stone?" asked Lydecker.

Stone thought for a moment, then he said, "Do you have any whisky?" Lydecker opened a drawer by his bunk and took out a bottle of Bourbon. Stone poured some onto his hands. "Got a match?" Lydecker obliged.

Stone lit his hands. Sheets of flame wrapped around each finger. Clouds of fire, yellow and red. Bright even in the bright room. He held them up like torches. "It's an old stuntman's trick," he said. "If they've got to burn in a movie, they rub themselves with alcohol. It burns a quarter of an inch clear of the skin thus doing no damage, unless you keep it up for too long."

He waved his hands in the air until they went out. Silence.

It was 0244 when the three of them landed. They beached the rubber craft silently. Gant glanced out to sea. "Hey, the ship's moving," he hissed. They all looked. The perspex windows of the Bell six-seater helicopter on the foredeck caught the starlight, turning. "Where's it going?" whispered Stone. Lydecker shrugged. They began to jog silently up the beach.

"AAAAAAaaaaaaggghh . . . h . . . h . . .!" A terrible scream.

"What was that!" Lydecker.

"Sssh!" Stone.

"By the waterfall," from Gant: the ghost of a whisper. Stone nodded. They crept forward again, swiftly and silently. Lydecker froze, arm pointing: two figures in the trees. They ran forward fast, silently, guns ready. They fanned out. The two figures stayed where they were. They closed in, crept up, working as a team as though with years of practice.

Easing in, until: "All right," said Lydecker. "Turn around slowly. No tricks."

Two strangers turned round. A medium-sized man, lean and hard, and a great shaggy bear who said in scarcely intelligible English. "We are officers from a Soviet submarine. We hear signal on radio and come lend aid . . ."

Then Lydecker's lights went on. "Do not move, please." From behind the glare.

"Wells. You . . .!" Gant swung round. A bullet kicked up the sand by his foot. "DON'T move, Mr Gant," said Silas Wells, the Hummingbird. Gant froze. "Very good. Now, throw your guns away, please." They did so. "Now,

190

sit down. Not you, Gant." Gant remained on his feet while the others sat carefully on the ground. "I hope for all your sakes you still have your body-belt on, Gant."

Gant said nothing. "*Well?*" snapped Wells, his voice cracking up with the strain on the word.

"Yes," said Gant.

"Take it off."

Gant pulled up his pullover and took the belt off. "Throw it here." He threw it. It flew heavy and flat into the dark, weighted by his treasured first edition of *Long Day's Journey into Night*.

"I'm going to kill you, Wells," said Gant.

"I think not. I think it will be the other way around."

Stone's back found a lamp-standard.

"Where would you like me to shoot you first, Gant?"

Stone pushed.

"In the leg, perhaps?"

Stone pushed harder.

"In the groin?"

God, it was heavy.

"In the belly, I think, to make up for my disappointment with Miss Dark . . ."

The lamp crashed over, pulling all the others with it. Dark. Wells began shooting, but nobody was where he had been in the light.

Beria found a gun, rolled on his back and began shooting at the point where the man called Wells had spoken from. But the Hummingbird had also moved: he and the Bee were running for the cliffs and the Bee's dinghy: two vague shapes in the moonlight.

The five began to run after them. Up the slope they sprinted, slipping, scrabbling, puffing fit to burst. Gant in the lead: he had no gun but he didn't care. Beria next, .38 Colt at the ready. The others close behind. Stone had a big Smith and Wesson .44 Magnum. Lydecker had another Colt and a torch. He was wondering where his .44 Magnum had gone. And so they raced up the whale's back hump of the island towards the cliffs. Hummingbird followed the Bee over to their right, towards the north-east cliffs. Each man's mind was deeply withdrawn, concentrating utterly upon running up the steep, treacherous slope.

The air began to shake.

They ran on, oblivious, each concentrating utterly upon his own special goal.

The air trembled, as though it were the ground quaking. Concussions of pressure thundered without sound upon their eardrums.

The pursuers began to slow. Hummingbird and Bee, highest still, a hundred yards ahead, froze. They were looking over the tall cliff edges, looking out to sea. Beria fired: the tall one sagged. They were almost up with them now . . .

But the air was like a deep bass organ note, full of hardly audible sound rushing majestically. Beria dropped on one knee. They were outlined against the distant sea. He could finish them now. He never fired.

Beyond the two men, beyond the cliffs, the ocean in the moonlight gathered itself up. The surface, slick and black, shining faintly, utterly unmarked by foam phosphorescence, whorl or bubble, rose gracefully and incredibly swiftly into the air. Beria caught a glimpse of a ship like a toy labouring up the face of the wave towards the oil-dark round of its crest. He had never seen anything like it. As far as the eye could see on either hand it rose up out of the obsidian ocean, and up and up and up.

"DOWN!" he screamed at last, but the word was indistinguishable from the sound. Maelstrom. The ground shook. Shuddered. Heaved, seeming to throw itself into the conflict as the wave struck.

It was perhaps 100 ft high when it crested a hundred yards out from the cliffs. It was moving at 500 mph. It washed over the lower parts of the island carrying away the two dinghies, the lights, the supplies, the camp, the bushes, the trees, the waterfall, the little cliff, without even a pause. It broke against the cliffs to the north. All of the men screamed as the sound exploded in their ears. The ground shuddered and heaved beneath their clawing fingers. A wall of spray exploded into the air, for a fraction of a second extending the cliff, as in a mirror, for three times its own height. The steady wind pushed much of the spray back out to sea, but still tons of water rained down upon them like boulders, sweeping them towards the cliff edge, smashing them, half drowning them, half killing them. Then it was gone.

The epicentre of the Indian earthquake had been some 20 miles offshore and the frenzied heaving of the ocean had caused three great waves to rise as though a giant had dropped monstrous boulders into the sea. They spread in great concentric circles down the coast of India, across to the coast of Africa, and, moving at nearly 500 mph, across the Indian ocean.

The waves themselves were the tips of huge wheels of underwater movement rolling south at this great speed. In deep water the wheels of movement sank so that the waves on the surface only rose 10 ft from trough to crest. A ship would hardly notice their passing if it was well prepared. A submarine would be destroyed in an undersea hurricane of unimaginable currents. But as the ocean bed sloped upwards into the Socotra-Chagos ridge, so the wheels of motion, pushed up by the bottom, in turn forced the surface into huge combers five, eight, ten times their original height.

Their leading surfaces steepened, for their impulse was

all forward. The steady wind gave them some sort of a prop on which to lean as they gained a few more dizzy feet. And the sound began as they caught the lower air against their towering surfaces and tore it into invisible inverted echoes of themselves. The friction between a sky that tried to remain static, the seabed which also tried to be inert, and millions of tons of water hurling across the face of the globe at these fantastic speeds set up notes, resonances, harmonics of incredible power. The sky heaved and the earth quaked anew.

But it was when they met land that the waters' true fury was unleashed.

Gant crawled to his feet, brought to movement by the strength of his fixation. Through the continuous explosion of thunder on the air, so powerful it hurt his lungs and was like an unceasing series of punches to his diaphragm, across the trembling semi-liquid ground, he began to run towards the inert forms of his enemies.

As he was the only person on his feet, he was the only person to see what happened next. The second wave, slowed by the friction as it gathered itself up the submarine ridge until it gained its final peak of 80 ft, was further slowed and steepened here by the backwash of the first. Up the massive black, spume-laced wall of its leading edge laboured a merchant-ship. It seemed to be sailing up the mountain of water at an incredible angle.

The sharp bow of the ship cleft the crest of the wave, seemingly almost level with the cliff edge, but obviously going to make it to safety, when an incredible thing happened. The third wave caught up. Briefly the great wheel of motion in the water rode up, not upon the rocky ridge in the seabed, but upon the slower wheel of the wave in front. What had been 80 ft magically became 150 ft. The ship began to slide back. The top half of the new wave

194

was still travelling faster than the bottom. It crested, like surf on a beach, and millions of tons of water began to cascade forward down the liquid slope. A boiling wall of white smothered the ship as a mill-race smothers a twig.

Gant was utterly stunned. He had seen the Niagara Falls many times and frankly this was not of the same height. But then Niagara did not stretch from horizon to horizon. He had never seen it from as close as this. And the Falls had never come roaring towards him at 400 mph, brandishing a full-sized freighter like a dagger at its shoulder. It was the most terrifying thing the actor had ever experienced. He threw himself full length on the soaking turf, burying his face in the salt-running grass stems and crossing his arms behind his neck, and pressing his forearms over his ears.

The noise that the first wave made was nothing compared with this. The cliff of water exploded against the cliffs of rock with such force that the whole island rocked. The *Glorious Revolution*, bow first, moving as fast as the water, hit the sheer rock face at the speed of a flying aircraft and exploded through the wall into the cave itself. In the cave, the pillars toppled. Water roared down the tunnels from the caverns in the cliffs. Water sprayed at pressure through cracks in the limestone walls. A hurricane of pressurised air whirled between the crumbling columns, carrying with it the bodies of Bates and Miss Buhl like pale leaves in autumn. A jet of spray roared like the breath of a blowing whale out of the tiny hole in the slope below the men, but none of them heard it. The roof of the dome cracked, splintered, settled. Boulders fell.

The island screamed. The water, pushed with the power of millions of tons in violent motion, plunged the wreck of the *Glorious Revolution* right through the cliff battering aside great slabs of limestone as though they had been a child's bricks and followed the ruined ship itself, until a column of pure water roared up out of the island's blowhole to meet the spray from the wave coming down.

And then it was gone. It re-formed behind the island in a wild hectare of whirlpools and white water. The sound died a little, but did not still, for the water in the cavern was now 200 ft above sea-level and it began to roar back out of the hole in the cliff like an enormous fire-hose, and the ground continued to quake.

Gant, monomaniac, was on his feet again, stumbling over the suddenly uneven ground towards the Hummingbird. He threw himself on the unconscious man and wrestled the body-belt from his hand. Wells was face-down. Gant turned him over, wanting in that savage moment to look into his eyes as he died. Wells' face was black and shiny. There was no hair and seemingly little skin. It was the face of a very fat man, puffed out obscenely by burns. Around the mouth the flesh was split into vivid red gashes. The ears were almost entirely gone. The nose seemed to have melted out of shape.

Gant staggered to his feet and began to move back, retching. On his hands lingered the sweet smell of roast meat. Wells stirred, groaned: salt water was like flames against his burns. His lips moved: "It all went wrong. All wrong . . ." Gant turned and began to stumble back towards the others. The roaring went on: the ground continued to tremble and heave.

Suddenly there was a blinding light from the sky. He froze, transfixed by its powerful glare. Then he shaded his eyes and looked up. Beyond the light, the shape of the Bell helicopter. Gant couldn't understand why it made so little noise. He began to run towards it, then something kicked his legs out from underneath him and he fell.

"There!" screamed Rebecca into Hannegan's ear. "I see Mr Gant." Then she choked into silence as the runner stumbled. She could not know that the Bee had shot him. The helicopter touched down like a dragonfly on a thin lilypad. Hannegan kept the engine running, ready to leap into the air at the first sign of trouble.

"OK," he said, his eyes on the sea. Rebecca leaped out to search for the three men they had come to rescue. She had insisted on coming and Hannegan, quirky as ever, had insisted she should do so in spite of wiser judgements.

Rebecca couldn't remember the ground being so terribly uneven. She fell several times because it was still shaking so badly. They had given her ear-mufflers against the helicopter's whine, so she missed the worst of the noise. Stone and Lydecker were lying close by, stunned and almost unconscious. Rebecca ran to them screaming, "Alec, Alec," until he stirred. "Get into the helicopter, Alec." Stone mumbled, still confused. "HURRY," she screamed.

Stone's mind began to clear. He pulled himself to his feet. Lydecker also was stirring. Rebecca helped them up and began to support them towards the helicopter. Stone was just climbing in when a bullet whipped viciously by his head. He swung round and dived away, knocking free a rope ladder as he did so.

Rebecca, noticing nothing of this, had gone looking for Gant and found two strangers instead. Stone could see her pulling them also to their feet. He felt a quick poignant stab of admiration for her, then he was running towards Gant. Lydecker put his head out of the helicopter's door and a bullet burned his deafened ear. On the far side of the island a grotesque shape arose, a shape with impossibly wide shoulders and no head, shooting wildly as it staggered towards the helicopter: the Bee, carrying his beloved Hummingbird.

Stone saw Gant getting up, waving him back, and turned to help Rebecca with the Russians. The Bee stopped shooting.

Gant was on his feet hobbling towards them. The group of four were at the helicopter, Rebecca in first, then the Russians. Nobody had a gun. Stone swung back. Gant was stumbling towards them. The Bee still more than 300 ft away. And suddenly the whole island gave a massive lurch.

In the cavern, what was left of the *Glorious Revolution* had been hurled by the last pressure of the water sideways – on through the cliff. Hannegan engaged the rotors automatically – the Bell leaped into the air. The rope ladder began to unroll. Stone caught it feverishly and just in time was jerked off the ground.

Behind the Bee the cliffs began to fall. Boulders of limestone began to tumble like great misshapen bricks from a wall. Immediately behind the cliffs, the first rank of rock slabs which made up the dome of the island itself, tilted and began to tumble towards the sea. And the next, tearing the turf, rearing suddenly into great steps 10 ft high as whole surfaces of the island, each, perhaps 300 ft square, slid away to tumble 200 ft into the seething ocean.

Gant was thrown to his face, then he was up again. "Back!" yelled one of the strangers – Andropov – to Hannegan. "Go back. Closer." His English was suddenly clear – and his tone irresistible.

Stone swung like a pendulum on the end of the ladder. The island had twisted away beneath him as the Bell leaped into the air, and he was over the ocean now. But he could still see the figures running, the far edge of the land collapsing.

The Bee was still going. He could not stop, he would not stop. The ground beneath his feet began to heave as though some buried giant were breaking free. The slab of rock he was running over began to tilt and fall out towards the sea. "No!" he screamed. With all his strength, the Bee swung his beloved Hummingbird off his shoulders. The ground in front of him began to rise. He went to his knees. He began to slide. Hummingbird, the beautiful Hummingbird, stirred. The Bee hurled the light wiry body of his love away towards safety with all his strength. But the strain was too much. His heart seized. "*Ngha!*" he cried and the ground smashed his face. Hummingbird fell close by. The tilt of the rock caused him to slide back until he lay beside the Bee. Together, entwined like lovers on a massive bed, they were hurled into the void.

Gant pounded towards the helicopter, swinging the body-belt recovered from Wells: the O'Neill. He was trying to save, not himself, but his priceless signed first edition of *Long Day's Journey into Night*. The slab under him began to tilt. A black mouth yawned beneath his feet. He stopped on the edge, began to slide back. The gap widened. Stone swung towards him on the rope ladder. Gant threw the belt carefully and Stone caught it with ease. Stone looked at him standing on the edge of a high cliff which was beginning to fall away.

"Jump!" he screamed. The helicopter moved daintily, and Stone was swinging towards the actor.

Gant looked up, helpless. The ladder was 20 ft away. Then 15, then 10. The ground lurched sickeningly. Gant staggered. The boulder began to fall.

"Jump!" screamed Stone, and Gant hurled himself, arms outstretched, over the roaring dark.

Part Three
Post Mortem

Aftermath

Indira was dying. Held unwaveringly by Ram, she had survived a night of terror and increasingly agonising cramps. She had survived the horror of aftershocks which had rumbled across the stricken province in the dark before the dawn. She had survived – miraculously – the soul-deep shame of the creeping daylight which revealed all too starkly their plight. But the sun was killing her inevitably and agonisingly with the unremitting weight of its terrible, furnace heat.

There had been no chance for them to turn and present Ram's back to the public scrutiny and the equally burning kiss of the sun. The tiny corner of flooring left beneath their feet was slippery and splintery. They had tried to move once, and only the strength of Ram's young shoulders wedged in the corner behind, the force of his arms and the power of his love had held them in place as they fought to regain their footing.

In the gathering dawn, with the suspicion of organised intelligence far below in the wreckage of Rajkot beginning to stir into audible life, they had called for aid; poor Indira torn agonisingly between desire to be rescued and horror at the thought of anyone seeing her in this state. But all they

203

had done was to exhaust themselves and add thirst to the other agonies with which they were clothed as their gasping cries sucked dust and smoke into their crying throats.

Increasingly hoarsely, between bouts of shouting, they had whispered endearments to each other – each one willing strength and fortitude into the other, hanging on grimly against all the odds. As the light gathered out of the east, however, and smote down like molten gold upon her head, shoulders and the outwards swell of her hips, Indira fell silent and concentrated on simply hanging on. She entered a kind of dream-world where it soon became impossible to distinguish vivid hope from distant reality. Sirens screamed in the distance like the voices of strange legendary creatures. Ram's hoarse breathing and increasingly monosyllabic endearments also retreated into the distance of her childhood dreams. All that was real was the discomfort in her twisted muscles, the pain in her feet, the blistering power of the sun, the piercing agony of her headache and the desert burning of her throat.

"I can't hang on any more," Indira whispered, vividly aware that her swollen tongue and lips were slurring words already reduced to a ghostly croak by the state of her dusty throat. "I'm sorry . . ."

As Indira's body began to slump outwards, Ram pulled back with the last of his strength so that he could fasten his dry, swollen lips to hers. The enormity of his love for her filled his chest to bursting and left no room for regrets or recriminations. At no time in any of the whispered words exchanged during their ordeal had there been any hint of bitterness. They might have blamed the ill fortune that had brought them to this place at this time. She might well have blamed him that they had not met a sudden but decorous end when their bed fell into whatever wreckage lay below and behind them. He certainly might have blamed himself for the fact that his desires and actions had brought them to this end. But there was no bitterness between them – only a loving strength which lasted for as long as it could and now had reached its end.

"I love you," he said as she slipped out of his arms. Since sunrise he had been saving the phrase for this moment, knowing in his heart of hearts that it would come.

He had wanted his protestation of love to be the first thing she heard on the first day of their new life – then he had wished it to be the last thing she ever heard him say. So, tearing his brick-kiln throat with the power of the force imprisoned in his cramp-wracked chest, he bellowed again "I love you!" and he flung himself wildly down after her.

And for a moment which seemed to linger eternally, he saw her spread like a falling star below him, her eyes wide, seeming to beckon him, her lips parted, calling something which the wild wind spreading her hair like a black web whipped away from her ears; arms reaching yearningly: all the pale loveliness of his beloved young wife, framed against the bright yellow circle of the emergency services' inflatable safety equipment which stood waiting to hold them safe.

Washington, November

Parmilee was tired to death. The Secretary of State took the top corner of the last page of the last file and slid it under the perfectly manicured nail of his right thumb. His eyes were on the dark-typed flimsy but he did not see it. His mind was elsewhere. Parmilee sat beside him, stunned with fatigue, numb from neck to knees. "I like the way you have sketched in the probable behaviour of other agencies at important points. Is that standard practice?"

"Depends," said Parmilee. He had stopped saying

"Mr Secretary" after everything a little before midnight.

"You were lucky no one minded being de-briefed," said the Secretary. "So many foreign nationals were involved."

"Yes," temporized the big agent, "but Ed Lydecker is an expert in that sort of thing, and we had just saved their lives."

The Secretary said, "Even so. The two Englishmen, Stone, and Nash when he healed up a bit. And the two Russians. We got away with one hell of a lot."

"No doubt of that, sir."

"Still. That's not what we're here about. That's not the central question at all. The central question is *why?*"

Taking the disparate files, interviews, case notes, prognostications, weather reports, ships' logs, they had welded the Action into a story. Now they began to break the story apart, looking at its heart: trying to discover what made it beat. And of course the first pulse, which began everything and then died itself, was Feng.

Feng had come out of China with something important which he wanted to use as a bargaining counter. He had not passed this to anyone in Hong Kong, of course: in a game of poker one does not open the bidding by saying, "I have four aces." This information, this bargaining counter, would have been revealed in due course to Lydecker or to Parmilee.

Feng still had it, therefore, when he realized that Hong Kong Local Station was not capable of protecting him. He kept it with him on his panicked run to Kai Tak and his flight to Singapore. He didn't run to Singapore for any reason other than that this had been the destination of the first flight he could get on. Nevertheless, perhaps in Singapore, perhaps on the aeroplane, he began to think. Therefore, some if not all of his actions in Singapore were dictated by reason.

He went to the *Wanderer* for a reason. He went aboard, spoke with no one, came a shore. And yet it was logical to assume that he had left his bargaining counter somewhere on the ship. The Chinese assumed he had done so, or Hummingbird would not have gone aboard. Hummingbird could not have found it, or he would not have tried to disable the engine. He had had weeks in which to search, and he was an outstanding agent so they could assume it was nothing obvious or easily accessible.

But they had more information than Hummingbird had: they had, for instance, an exhaustive list of Feng's purchases in Singapore, for each transaction in which he had used his credit card had been carefully recorded. With dull eyes they went down the list, comparing it with the case notes supplied by the three agents from Singapore Local Station. Bank, food shop, clothes shop, book shop, shoe shop, another food shop and so forth, and so on.

"He bought a newspaper," said the Secretary.

"*Straits Times*," Parmilee read it off the list.

"Can we get a copy?"

"I don't know. We could try Records. They might have a copy on file." His voice was doubtful.

"Try."

Parmilee rang through to Langley. They were lucky. Sections of the paper had been micro-copied. "Why?" asked the Secretary, as the microcopy and a microcopy reader were being rushed to them by the night staff. "Articles about American VIPs," said Parmilee. The Secretary nodded. Within half an hour the microcopy reader was before them, its television face flooding like the dawn sky into silvery brightness. The paper had been copied by authority of Chief of Station, Singapore. Copies appended to the file on Feng's Defection (Action unnamed). Copies to Records, and Ex-Serviceman File:

Eldridge Gant (Special Forces – MATA Dept. Ref. 1965–9).

The whole of three pages had been copied. Page one, which contained a news story about Eldridge Gant. Page eight which contained an interview with the actor, and page fifteen with a review of his one-night charity performance of *Macbeth*. On page one, the headline (a small sub-head part way down column four) read 'ACTOR REVEALS I WAS SPECIAL FORCES HERO.' It was a front page filler story, blown up a little to lift it from being gossip into being news. On page eight Gant's actual involvement was more fully examined. It was not as sensational as the front page seemed to promise, but it might be enough to offer hope to a terrified defector, fleeing for his life. On page 15 a rave review of Gant's performance ended by revealing that he was in the process of returning to America in order to act in Eugene O'Neill's *Long Day's Journey into Night*, a play which he had never tackled before, although he considered it 'the finest play since Shakespeare. A work of the greatest genius'. Immediately below Gant's fulsome praise of the play, there was a quarter-page advertisement for a large westernised bookshop in the Queenstown district offering a range of volumes from cheap paperbacks to priceless First Editions.

Both men understood at once. It must have seemed like a gift from God to the terrified defector. His one wish was to get rid of his bargaining counter – for if Hummingbird and Bee found it on him, then they would take that back and leave Feng himself behind, probably floating in the Singapore Roads. Simply to throw it away would leave him defenceless if he escaped and re-established contact with CIA.

What he did smacked of genius. He bought the rarest edition of O'Neill's play that he could find, secreted his secret bargaining counter somewhere within it and sent it to a man who first would treasure the gift and secondly, as an ex-serviceman, would be capable of protecting the secret he didn't even know he held, if anything went wrong.

The Secretary of State slammed his telephone to his ear and said to the switchboard, "Get me Eldridge Gant. His suite at the Waldorf. I know what the time is, dammit! Just get me Eldridge Gant." He covered the mouthpiece with a broad hand and said, "Twenty minutes! That's incredible. I don't know which of them should get an award: Gant or Alec Stone, but to hang on to the bottom rung of a ladder like that for twenty minutes – even with someone holding your wrist – that's incredible." Then his eyes abruptly lost focus, his hand moved and he said, "Eldridge? Hello, Eldridge? Look, I know it's a hell of a time, but listen . . ."

Beijing, December

The Chairman was dying, but even so he had come to 15 Bowstring Alley himself. He had one last matter of overwhelming importance to discuss with the quiet but infinitely powerful men who occupied the top floor here.

"If we need a name for the action," observed the Chairman, his voice a broken whisper, "we will call it 'Action: Chairman's Legacy'."

The Director of the Social Affairs Department sat quietly, nodding. His face, surprisingly fine-boned for a Chinese, was expressionless. "There are only a few more gestures to be performed," continued the Chairman. "We must look for some suitably humiliating act which we can perform with regard to Russia."

"There is that pilot who may or may not have been photographing our defences before he crashed well within our territory," said the Director. "Might we not return him to his family and loved ones?"

"Yes indeed. That would be perfect. An unexpected, unsolicited diplomatic courtesy. Perfect. The Kremlin and the FSS will know for certain that Washington has something capable of throwing us into utter confusion." The two men laughed.

The barbarian President and the Gweilo 'Foreign Devil' – Secretary of State had returned to America the day before. Their visit to Beijing had been a notable success for the American policy of detente. Without upsetting Moscow too much, the President had quite obviously extended a hand of gracious friendship towards the Peoples' Republic. And the hand had been warmly accepted.

Those who had looked upon the President's mission with some misgiving after the humiliation of the Secretary of State at the hands of the same men scant weeks earlier, breathed covert sighs of relief and looked wisely at each other. The Secretary had got something on the yellow devils, they said: the cunning old bastard had found his big stick.

Tucked neatly, immovably and invisibly into the spine of Eldridge Gant's priceless signed First Edition of Eugene O'Neill's *Long Day's Journey into Night* was a piece of tissue paper covered with Chinese characters.

It had been inevitable in the new political climate that the Social Affairs Department should consider breaking with centuries of tradition and begin a series of Intelligence Actions designed to prepare the new battlefields for the re-emerging Dragon Empire. Making full use of the five types of spy enumerated by Sun Tzu, the Director at the behest of the ailing Chairman, had arranged an action whose prime objective had been to distract the other major forces threatening the Peoples' Republic.

Although Sun Tzu himself had been primarily concerned

with wars between the same racial types, his strictures proved wise guidance for men running actions across racial boundaries. The SAD had, therefore, sought native spies from among the ranks of their enemies, and internal spies from among their officials to supply the native spies with information, to run and guide them. Double spies purchased with the liberality suggested by *The Art of War*. Doomed spies, such as Feng was designed to be, and returning spies such as Hummingbird and Bee had been supposed to be – had various forces beyond even the SAD's control not doomed them after all.

But, with the patience and the deviousness upon which the whole Chinese People justly pride themselves, the Action had only started here – and as it proceeded, so it gained a truly oriental elegance. For the SAD had begun to target men and women who could move from one end of the crumbling Soviet Empire to the farthest reaches of San Francisco without arousing suspicion. Men who could be called upon – if the call were carefully framed – to perform a range of acts guaranteed to preoccupy their unsuspecting hosts. There was almost an inevitability about the conjoining of a militantly non-religious state and the power of uncontrolled fanaticism.

Secretly but surely, the SAD began to purchase with a range of things far more subtle than money the allegiance of a series of Moslem leaders. The majority of these good men, each with their own burning agenda, remained ultimately unaware precisely who was fulfilling their wishes. It was impossible, after all, to tell a Kalashnikov made in Moscow from a perfect replica manufactured in Manchuria; to discriminate between Semtex made in Czechoslovakia and China. From Afghanistan to Chechnya, from Trabzon to the World Trade Centre, the Ayatollahs followed their individual agendas and the SAD supplied their needs.

211

There was only one list of the names and contacts by which this process had been facilitated. One flimsy sheet of almost rice-thin paper, covered in black Chinese script; and this had been Feng's bargaining counter. The list of all the Muslim militants supplied by the Social Affairs Department, and their materiel, command structures, main bases, had gone south with Feng all those weeks ago. It had passed through Hong Kong in the days before that colony became Xiang Gang once more and had vanished in Singapore. Folded into the spine of *Long Day's Journey into Night*, it had gone with Eldridge Gant into the lifeboat and onto the island; to New York and finally to Washington, onto the desk of the Secretary of State.

In the face of this, the Chairman was, of course, powerless. Everything the Secretary suggested, everything the President mentioned became matters of the utmost moment. The President's visit was a triumph for the United States. Feng's list, said the Secretary of State, would be buried in files far beyond the reach of the most assiduous, or powerful, searcher.

Now the Chairman sat with the Director of the SAD in a modest room, high in No. 15 Bowstring Alley. "It has all passed off excellently," said the Chairman. "The seed is sown. There has been enough blood to nurture it. Now all it needs is time. Life will not trouble me much longer. I will allow myself, therefore, the old man's perogative of prognostication if not of outright prophesy.

"What we have given the Americans, the list of the Muslim activists, is a poisoned chalice, a time bomb. They try to pursue a policy of peace and understanding between both our nations, yet we are almost at war, the Peoples' Republic and Russia. They can only remain in friendship with us, therefore, if they do not reveal what is written on Feng's paper to our enemies. And if the Russians ever find out that at a time of understanding and detente between Washington and the Kremlin, the USA held the list and did *not* tell them about it, they will never forgive the Americans.

"And they *will* find out, of course, perhaps not tomorrow, but eventually . . ."

"In American politics, tomorrow is a long way away," observed the Director, with the voice of a man advised by a strategist who had lived 2,500 years ago.

"In life, Mr Director, five years are nothing. The blink of an eye. Yes, I would guess that five years would see it done. In five years they will be at each others' throats. No matter who is in each White House, no matter who rules in Langley and in the Lubianka, they will be tearing each other to pieces and we will be free to do as we wish, economically, politically, militarily . . ."

The old man fell silent and leaned back in the simple chair, his eyes narrow and his thin lips wide as he smiled the smile of the tiger.

London, July

The prince was dying but he did not know it yet. Nash leaned forward until his still healing side began to protest, his whole being enraptured by the sight as never before. Perhaps it was the production; perhaps it was the occasion. Perhaps it was the medication.

"How does the Queen?" asked the prince, gasping, his face alive with concern and awash with perspiration. Nash unconsciously narrowed his eyes and drew shuddering breaths. He would never have begun to dream that Alec Stone could pull off a performance as intense as this.

"She swoons to see them bleed," laughed the stricken King in half answer, glancing round the gleaming, jewel-bright court with a wildness only the camera saw – only the wide screen revealed. The Dolby quadraphonic system brought every rich resonance of Gant's rolling dramatic voice and showed how completely he had sunk himself into the part. Not a trace of the Irish-American of his towering James Tyrone.

And the Queen – only Gant could have persuaded her to play the part – pulled her sinking body up to look upon her panting nephew-son. "No, no, the drink, the drink! Oh my dear Hamlet, the drink, the drink . . ."

Nash tore his eyes away from the agony on the screen and looked across the Royal box past Rebecca Dark and Alec Stone to where Eldridge Gant was sitting beside the real Prince. The American's distinguished profile was alive with revelation and the old spy realized with a lurch that Gant had not seen himself on celluloid since before he went to Viet Nam.

Words whirled out of the speaker system, washing over the entranced Royal Premier audience whose clothes were scarcely less glittering than the courtly gorgeousness upon the screen.

"Thy mother's poisoned. I can no more. The King! The King's to blame . . ."

Soldier Nash shook his head in wonder and looked back up just in time to see Alec Stone – no, not Alec at all; Prince Hamlet – jump over the body of the fainting Laertes and hurl himself upon the shrinking figure of the King. The poisoned sword point drove home and the dying monarch howled. Nash recognized that sound. He had been told about it at length. It was the cry the Bee had made on seeing what was left of the burned Hummingbird.

Jaw squared, wild face working, Hamlet snatched the poisoned chalice from the rigid fingers of his dead mother and hurled himself back on the King. Blood welled out of the

214

royal mouth. Poisoned wine choked in, the one as gloriously ruby as the other. "Follow my mother," screamed the crazed young man, and his uncle's bloodshot eyes rolled up.

Horatio gently pulled the fainting Prince to his feet and they gasped a broken conversation as Laertes died and Hamlet followed into silence.

Young Fortinbras strode onto the scene and surveyed the carnage with lordly disdain. He spoke to Horatio and the courtiers, then spat his orders to his men. Such was his assumption of command that old Soldier felt his wounded body jumping to obey.

The wide, wide camera pulled back. The exquisite setting became framed and still, like a Rubens or a Raphael. "Take up the body," ordered Fortinbras, his voice growing as distant as the gorgeous scene. "Such a sight as this becomes the field but here shows much amiss. Go, bid the soldiers shoot . . ."

Music swirled. Credits rolled. The audience rose.

Nash found himself on his feet with all the rest, looking with something akin to awe at the faces of Alec Stone and Eldridge Gant. It seemed incredible to him that they should have taken Broadway by storm and still have found time – the resources – to make a film as powerful as this. It was, thought Soldier Nash, as much of a miracle as all the rest.

And, as he clapped until he thought his hands would bleed and watched the tears spill out of Rebecca's laughing eyes, the screen, reflected in the lenses of Eldridge Gant's spectacles filled with two words:

'The End'.